Speak Easy

A TALE FROM THE EFFLUVIUM

E.S. Barrison

E.S. Barrison
www.esbarrison-author.com

Publisher's Note: This is a work of fiction. Names, characters, places, and incidents are a product of the author's imagination. Locales and public names are sometimes used for atmospheric purposes. Any resemblance to actual people, living or dead, or to businesses, companies, events, institutions, or locales is completely coincidental.

Book Layout © 2017 BookDesignTemplates.com
Cover designed by MiblArt

Speak Easy: A Tale from the Effluvium/E.S. Barrison. -- 1st ed.
ISBN 979-8-9853634-1-8

Dedicated to anyone who is afraid to tell their story.

Your story is worth telling.

And I'll always be there to listen.

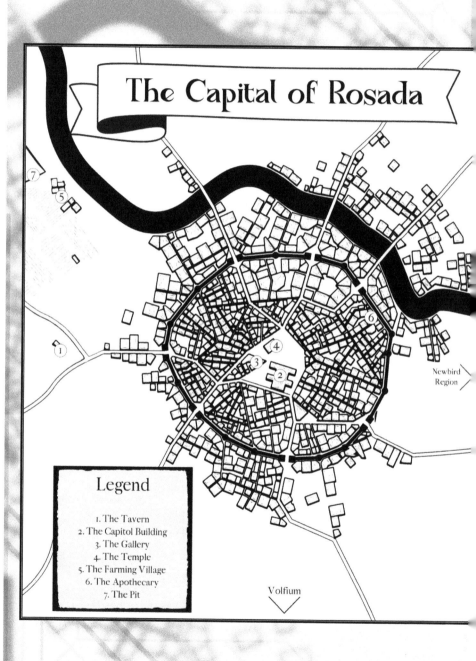

The Capital of Rosada

Newbird Region

Legend

1. The Tavern
2. The Capitol Building
3. The Gallery
4. The Temple
5. The Farming Village
6. The Apothecary
7. The Pit

Volfium

ONE

.----

Father died soon after my nineteenth birthday on a day when the misty hands of Death's Grip flooded the swamp beneath my home. The stories go that if someone dies when Death's Grip is at its strongest, then they won't suffer. And like so, Father passed while asleep, a smile on his face, embracing his new death as an old friend. A day later, I lay his body to rest at the base of the Old Cypress Tree...alone.

That was that day I realized I had to leave Stilette, the city on stilts where I'd spent my whole life.

Memories haunted my home. In my adolescence, I played in the swamp, telling stories to my dolls made of sticks and moss while throwing mud balls at the neighborhood children. We would hide behind the stilts, watching as strangers performed feats of magic for our entertainment until our parents called from the boardwalks above to come and eat dinner. My mother would greet us with an ugly casserole after a day erecting the stilts that kept the city afloat, kissing both my sister and me on the head. At night, we gathered at my father's feet, listening to the stories he wove for the neighborhood children while teaching us all to read and write. Every night, as he told his stories, he tapped his foot in rhythm. Each beat was a different letter, each connection a different word.

These stories, mixed with his unusual tapping, left a twang in my heart. A desire for adventure, an urge to escape the now-empty home and see the world.

Just like my sister had a few years earlier.

So, I sold the house and packed a bag. The plan was simple: once the thickest plumes of Death's Grip left Stilette, I would hop on a caravan to Rosada, the nation north of my home.

Rosada wasn't my first choice to make a home, but it was the one place where I knew I wasn't alone. My sister moved there years ago to attend the prestigious Rosadian Academy. Every month, I received a telegraph using the all too familiar tap-code from her, begging that I come join her and her partner after she stopped her studies.

.—- —- .. -. / — .

"Join me," it said. "We have plenty of room."

With Father gone, nothing much held me back.

Yet, the rumors about Rosada worried me. Whenever travelers came through from the north, they bore no tales upon their lips, often keeping their heads down as local theater troops produced plays of swamp monsters and heroes in our streets. As a young girl, I thought it was because of the language barrier. When I asked my father about it, he never really had much of an answer. All he ever said was, "Some people believe stories taint the world and produce a false narrative. We do not. So, my Nanette, love your stories...for others cannot."

I only hoped what he said did not apply to Rosada as I prepared my bag to join a caravan heading north. But what did I have in Stilette otherwise? My mother had died years ago in an unfortunate construction accident. My sister had left a few years later and, now married, had no aspiration to return. Most of my childhood friends left Stilette seeking adventure and riches abroad. My father had been my confidante, my best friend; without him, I couldn't stay.

And even if I wanted to, the city was stagnant with no work that inspired me.

What stories were there to tell?

My father planted a yearning to grow in my heart. He wanted more for my sister and me than a life surrounded by swamp gas. Every day, growing up, he told us, "Elodie, Nanette, there's a bird on our windowsill. See it?" Sometimes, there wouldn't be a bird, but we would agree. "I want you to fly away someday like that beautiful bird."

He said it with such romance and grace. And, as soon as Elodie turned eighteen, she took his advice and flew away to Rosada to pursue her studies. Two years her junior, I stayed behind with our father, ignoring my own flourishing desires. He further declined after my mother's unprecedented death, whispering that he saw her in Death's Grip.

In his final days, he sometimes even confused me with my mother before launching into a fantasy about dragons. He would tell me, his eyes wide, to climb upon a dragon and leave this petty life to the mist. Other times, he claimed Death would arrive on a tremendous stork for him, and it would be his turn for an adventure.

After I gave his body over to the Old Cypress Tree, I sent a telegraph to Elodie saying I would join her in Rosada. Within three weeks, she'd used her connections to gain the proper documentation. She had a way of working the system despite never finishing her law degree, more enthralled with the adventures in the capital of Rosada than her own studies.

The day the papers arrived, I gathered them in my arm and read through each document carefully.

On top of them all, Elodie had inscribed a letter in her looped handwriting.

Doris –

I am so excited for you to join me in the Capital of Rosada! I have missed you dearly. There is so much I need to tell you that can't be summed in a single letter or a telegraph. That can all wait, of course.

Marietta and I have already prepared your room. Oh, I guess I haven't told you about Marietta, have I? That's right, I have a wife now! She started her transition last month, and we are so much happier.

Enough of that, though. We'll have all the time in the world to catch up.

In the meantime, all the legal documents you need are in this envelope.

I can't wait to see you!
Elodie

After reading through the letter twice, making sure to commit Elodie's wife's name to memory, I removed the legal documents. Upon reading them, I took my fountain pen and signed each document with my full name: *Doris Nanette Ivans.*

A single signature sealed my emigration from Stilette, and by the next morning, I hopped on a caravan north to pursue my new life.

The caravan I joined whisked me into a brand-new world. It consisted of an odd bunch who took in refugees and orphans, with a shared goal to see the world. They sang songs and told stories around their fires each night, all of them promising one thing: a chance.

There was something oddly enchanting about them. They cast a spell over me, displaying small feats of magic in the palms of their hands while painting stories with their music. I marveled as one traveler turned the fire different colors with a snap of his finger and another performed slights-of-hand with a deck of cards. To be honest, if I hadn't promised Elodie I would join her in the Capitol, I might have continued traveling.

The caravan gave me a chance to cut away the final threads tying me to my father and Stilette. As a child, I kept my head down, always obeyed the rules. I was naïve, pious, kind, and pure. Not once did I disobey orders, even if a fire brewed in my chest to shout.

Traveling with this caravan changed all that. I expanded my vocabulary, tasting the most obnoxious words in both the Rosadian language and my native tongue, Volfi.

"Damn."

"Bitch."

"Shite."

The first time I tried speaking those words while sitting around the fire with a few other travelers, they tasted bitter. But like a deep swig of ale, over time, the flavor grew familiar, and I treated them like any other words.

The curses unlocked another side of me. I cast aside the poise and grace I'd displayed for my father, letting my shoulders relax and my smile brighten. I opened myself up to some travelers, keeping most conversations short, while other times enamored with the stories around the fire.

I also began spending more time with a tall, striking woman named Gisela and a stout chiseled fellow named Yeshua. They took me under their wing, teaching me more curse words and telling stories of lives that might have sprawled centuries. Something drew me to them, their beauty making my heart flutter and causing warmth to rise in my chest.

About two weeks into my journey, I sat with them by the fire as we did most nights. Yeshua strummed along on his oud, a string instrument from his homeland abroad. Gisela told me stories about magic, talking about seers who saw the dead and a woman who saw heat. I scoffed. The story was anticlimactic, nowhere near as special as the dove catchers in Stilette or the traveler I'd met who turned his fingers invisible.

"Now, Nanette, there are many kinds of magic!" Gisela said.

"Yes, but seeing heat? That is so *fucking* uncreative." The curse formed a knot on my tongue.

Gisela balked. "Oh, how adorable she is! Did you see the way her face twisted when she cussed?"

Yeshua agreed, patting my hand. "It is quite adorable. She is innocent as a flower."

I blushed. Gisela and Yeshua's laughter made my heart swarm with a thousand different emotions, the types that are indescribable unless you feel them. Their smiles were flawless, eyes like jewels; they were almost like two gods carved perfectly out of stone, complementing one another in unison. Whenever they spoke, my attention fell only on their lips. Each chime of laughter left my head swimming.

And they were more perceptive than I knew.

Throughout our voyage, I'd been sneaking glances, trying my best to hide my internal attraction. But that night, beneath the moonlit sky, Gisela and Yeshua showed their true awareness.

As I tried to hide my flushing face, I continued to practice that confounded word. "Fuck." I didn't notice at first as the two of them shifted beside me until they were so close, I felt their breath against my skin. Gisela lifted her slender hand and pushed back my hair. When I raised my eyes to meet her gaze, Yeshua took my hand, tracing the veins on my wrist.

"Doris," Gisela whispered.

"Please, call me Nanette. I hate that name... *Doris*." I muttered.

"Nanette... yes, that is much prettier." She cupped my cheek. "Like you. You are so beautiful, Nanette."

My entire body stiffened as a heat bubbled in my belly. I'd felt this longing before, the warmth, the need, back when I was just piquing into womanhood and began stealing glances at others my age. Elodie told me it was all natural. She told me to guide myself through that warmth, to touch where my desires flourished, and let my body fly.

Like most adolescents, I'd experimented, but not enough to share the experience with someone else. What if I fell too deep into my desires? What if I didn't want to stop?

Now, with Gisela and Yeshua as my guides, I longed to explore the depths of my sacred core.

"You're so innocent...so young," Gisela continued. "You really haven't experienced the world yet, have you?"

"I want to," I replied as another spike of warmth lashed through my body. Yeshua's fingers had moved from my arm, down my stomach, and onto my thigh.

Gisela's lips were close to my ear now, brushing the edge of my skin. "Do you want us to help you learn?"

"I do." We had spent so much time together. I felt like they knew everything about me. Who else could I trust to teach me the art of desire?

I gasped as Yeshua's fingers navigated the area between my thighs, merely touches away from an area I deemed sacred. He was a man of a few words, but his movements spoke volumes.

I stared at Gisela as I spoke. She was stunning in the moonlight. "I want this..."

"Of course you do." Gisela unlaced my bodice.

Then, the pair lowered me onto the ground and taught me things about my body I never even fathomed.

I would never say that my sensuous affair with Gisela and Yeshua turned me into a woman. No. Not at all. I was a woman long before I cut myself loose of the tethers over my sexuality. What it did, though, was solidify the last bit of confidence and determination that had been brewing since my father passed away. It put a bow on everything.

I was independent now. Free. I did not have to meet expectations or do something because it would make my father happy. I could finally be me. If I wished to have sex, curse at the top of my lungs, or try on that uninhibited outfit hanging in a shop window, no one stopped me. I was my own person.

But, as we traveled through Rosada to the Capitol, I noticed a change not just in myself but in the atmosphere. Each city and town we passed through felt bleaker than the last, Death's Grip more like a storm cloud than an incandescent embrace. Shops sat with dark windows, and people strode through the streets with their heads bowed. People didn't gossip or smile, in contrast to the friendly streets of Stilette. I was a foreigner, not just in my accent but in my behavior as well.

If Stilette were a color, it would have been green.

But Rosada was gray.

And I was like a stain on its traditions.

The Capitol emerged on the horizon, glowering over evergreen forests and shrub-filled fields. It bore fear in its gaze, watching me as I approached with the caravan.

On the final night, I hid in the back of a wagon with Gisela and Yeshua, making love for the last time just out of sight from the Capitol's glare. I cried in their arms, my fear and heartbreak rocking every corner of my body. I couldn't believe it. In less than a day, I would no longer have these two wonderful people in my life. We'd spent so many hours together, touching, kissing, and uniting. But they did not need to stay with me in Rosada.

And I'd made a promise to my sister.

Wandering: that was their life. I was but one of many lovers on their adventure.

Not that I held any disdain. They had opened a whole new world to me.

The next morning, after a night of little sleep and many kisses, they walked with me into the Capitol, past the Guards in stone watchtowers. I gripped both their hands tight, my stomach twisting in knots and throwing bile into my throat.

At the marble archway to the plaza, Yeshua turned to me and said, "Doris Nanette?"

His voice startled me, but I stared into his face, memorizing his chiseled jawline all the same. "Yes?"

"Listen to me closely." He squeezed my hand. "Destiny does not control you. The people in your life are merely threads in your design. But they alone do not embroider it. You do. I can see you, Nanette, and I know you will do great things."

I shrunk. "But I don't know how..."

"You will learn." Yeshua kissed my fingertips. "You will be great."

Gisela placed her hand on the small of my back, "Our time with you has ended, dearest Nanette."

I shook my head, restraining tears. "I'm going to miss you both so much..."

"It is time to move on," Gisela said, then kissed me. Yeshua followed suit, his own lips lingering just as Gisela's did.

I clamored for them, but they pushed me into the crowds. They concluded their story with a wave, turned their back to me, and strode away as if on a cloud, leaving me alone in the heart of the Capitol, unsure how to begin my story.

TWO

..- - -

As soon as Yeshua and Gisela left, my shield cracked.
Certainly, everyone stared at me: I was a foreigner here,
dressed in a green chemise, my hair pulled back in an
unkempt braid and face beaten with dirt. I quivered beneath the watchful eye of the hourglass structure
perched upon the Temple in the City Center. It counted
each moment, jewels toppling from the upper chamber
into the one beneath it. The guards watched me with
similar intent from their towers and street corners. Rosada's gaze never ceased.

Even as I hailed a horse and buggy, I felt their gazes,
set aware by my thick accent cutting open my disguise.

It was clear.

I was not Rosadian.

Now, everyone would know. The Guard. The civilians.
Everyone.

But even as I climbed into the buggy, I kept my head
high.

"Where ya heading?" the cabby asked.

I handed him my letter from Elodie. He read it over, smirked, then gave it back to me.

"You going to Ms. Lieu's house? That's gonna cost ya a pretty penny. It's on the outskirts of the city, y'know."

I removed a small parcel of coins Elodie sent me. The cabby sifted through the coins, smiled, and pocketed them.

After I climbed aboard, with a thrust of the reigns, the cabby ushered his brown horse forward down the path. I sank back into the seat, holding my breath as the horse trotted over each bump and swerve in the road.

I kept my attention locked on the Capitol. It towered in a way that dwarfed Stilette. Buildings rose above the trees, buggies ran through the streets, and steam engines puffed clouds of smoke over the rooftops from the train tracks to the south. The watchtowers marked the landscape, peering through the heavy smog as if they constantly watched my every movement and thought.

In the Capitol, the smoke and guard existed as constant companions. The smoke left an ethereal glow about the buildings while the Guard waited on every corner with their bronze uniforms and unsmiling faces. Just seeing them standing there, as frigid and linear as the designs on the buildings, left a foul taste in my mouth.

Keeping my voice low, I leaned forward to ask the cabby, "Are there always so many guards?"

"They're usually out and about, but not usually like this." The cabby gripped the reins of his horse tight. "Think it's 'cause the new Senate is taking seat today or something. Not that I would call it much of a *new* senate, but eh, whatever, y'know? Same old, same old. People don't like change. As my pa says, people always change horses midstream, and we end up with shit like this."

"Change horses midstream?" I echoed.

"Y'know, they don't make good decisions, so we get stuck with the same senators time and time again, and nothing changes. You ain't from here, right? So you probably don't know much about this, do ya?"

"Oh, no, not really."

"Let me tell ya then..." The cabby ranted. In that short ride to Elodie's home, I learned everything about the Rosadian government...not that I remembered most of it. He told me about the elections every five years, where unchallenged senators formed dynasties across the country. He named each senator without having to think, his eyes lighting up with each detail. His excitement buzzed over different names, fixating on a senator from a mountain region as well as a few in the south. I couldn't keep up with all the names, but that didn't matter. His enthusiasm was contagious.

The cabby was a young fellow, probably a couple years older than me, with gorgeous hazel eyes and uneven stubble. His puffy red hair stuck out from beneath his large hat, as fiery as his personality. Like a flame, he flickered back and forth as he spoke.

And I hung onto every word, smiling when he laughed, trying my best to understand his jokes and metaphors.

"So, I gotta ask," the cabby said. "What brings you to Rosada and Ms. Lieu and all?"

"Oh, Ms. Lieu's my sister. I'm moving in with her."

"Guess I'll see ya around then. I'm one of the few cabbies who'll venture out this far."

"Why's that?"

"I don't live in the city, so I pass by here a lot, but a lot of cabbies don't think it's worth it to come out here. Not many people and kind of...dusty, y'know. Most cabbies prefer the glamor of the city. Not that Ms. Lieu blends in with the dust. She sticks out like a sore thumb, always garnished in the finest clothes. Wouldn't have thought of you as her sister. You got the same Volfium accent and all, but it's just that you don't look like her or anything." His face turned redder than his hair. "I don't mean that in a bad way! You're just...you're very pretty!"

I flushed. Usually, I would have shied away from a stranger's compliments, but this cabby had opened his heart and soul to me in a matter of seconds. He cast me in a net of stories and reeled me into his tales. To be frank, he wasn't a bad looking man either.

I stopped myself short of saying anything, though. My heart still bled from my goodbye with Gisela and Yeshua. This man was just a cabby I might never see again.

I didn't even know his name!

"Listen, um…" The cabby fumbled as he pulled up in front of a wide wooden house with more windows than steps. "If you ever want someone to show you around the Capitol, once you're all settled and such, just ask for me. I'm happy to give you the grand tour."

"That might be hard without a name," I noted.

"Oh, right! Sorry! My name is Ryon Barnes. If that's too hard, just think to yourself, 'If I were to house animals, what would I be?'… 'I'm a barn.'" He half chuckled at his poor joke. "Sorry…I don't know why I said that."

I smiled. "I'll remember, Ryon Barnes."

"Oh, good. Good."

I hopped off the back of the cabby and smiled at Ryon. "I'm Nanette, by the way."

"Nanette…" Ryon's cheeks reddened again. "Nanette…who is darker than a brunette…who smiles like a sunset."

"Mr. Barnes, I don't think now is the time for flirtation!" I stifled a giggle.

He shook his head. "I apologize. My mind is truly peculiar, and I am uncertain what I'm doing half the time."

"I like it." I grinned. "Hopefully I'll see you around, Mr. Barnes."

"You too, Nanette. You too."

He smiled one last time, showing off the golden tooth glistening in the back of his mouth. Then, with a single "hi-yah," he rode off down the road back towards the city.

My stomach churned, watching him go; would he find another girl like me to charm with his smile and lame jokes? Why did it matter? I had only met this young man. Plus, the whole time I spent with Yeshua and Gisela, not once was I jealous of their true romance. What was I thinking? I hardly knew Ryon Barnes, but here I was, watching him ride off with my hiccoughing heart.

I convinced myself it was just me clinging to companionship, the first friendly face in the vast stone jungle of the Capitol. It was best to forget about him. There were swarms of people to meet.

And for now, it was time to reunite with my sister.

"DORIS!" Elodie squealed as soon as she opened the door.

"I go by Nanette now..." I fidgeted as she threw her arms around me.

"Right, of course. Nanette. That is much nicer than that other name."

Elodie and I, for all intents and purposes, were complete opposites. Where I was quiet, she was loud. While I tanned easily, she burned; while my hair was black, hers was blonde; while my nose was big and pointed, hers was round and buttoned; while I was tall and round, she was short and thin; while my eyes were hazel, hers were green. But Father always said we had the same smile and often wrung our hands in the same ways that made everyone notice we were indeed sisters.

"Oh, darling! I am so happy to see you!" She squeezed me tight. "I would have come down for Daddy's funeral, but the cost and the timing were not ideal. Travel for me right now wouldn't be good. Oh, not at all. Plus, we had to get everything ready for you to come. I couldn't leave Marietta here alone either, the poor dear."

Elodie patted my cheeks. "Come! You must meet Marietta! She is wonderful! It is a shame you and Daddy didn't make it to our wedding a few months ago. I know, I know—cost! Pah! Money is always an issue, isn't it? And Daddy wasn't doing well. I am glad you made it, though...although it took you far longer than I would have hoped. You should have told me about your financial situation! I could have arranged something so you could have taken a train rather than a filthy caravan..."

She snatched my bag from me, continuing to babble as we walked inside the house. "Never mind that! You're here now! And now you're a part of me and Marietta's life! It will be so great, especially once...well...forget it. We can talk about it later. How was your journey from the city? Did the cabby get you here well? I hope—"

My mind wandered. I'd forgotten how much Elodie talked!

My attention drifted over the fixtures of the home while she showed me around. It was a sizeable house with a rickety stairwell leading to a basement containing old furniture and dusty bottles. A kitchen sprawled above the stairwell, and beside it, a comfortable parlor gazed over the front yard. A rifle hung on the wall amongst the bookshelves. Five bedrooms waited upstairs, with two bathrooms shared between them, as well as a half-sized lavatory downstairs. It reminded me much more of a tavern than a home.

Elodie finished giving me the grand tour, dropping my bags off at the foot of the stairs, before leading me back into the parlor. Elodie called into the room as we entered, "Marietta! Look! Doris is here! But don't call her Doris—call her Nanette. That is her name now."

Marietta looked up from her spot by the window. She smiled sanguinely at me, fixed her glasses, then turned back to the glass panes with a hollow stare. Her dark, empty eyes took me aback; how could my boisterous sister be with someone so quiet and disinterested? Elodie was the type of person to laugh at every bird fluttering by or fixate on the details of a doily on the end table. I expected her spouse to be similar.

I didn't ponder it for long, though. Elodie gripped me by the hands and spun me around in a circle, giggling like a schoolgirl.

"I am delighted you're here, Dor—Nanette! I missed you dearly, and I cannot wait to show you every corner of the Capitol. It makes Stilette feel minuscule, really! This...THIS is a city! We don't have people living under stilts or constant fires from ill performances or meals that are always mashed with fish! Disgusting, yes?" She laughed. "Oh, we have so much catching up to do! How is that neighborhood boy I used to like? I don't even remember his name. Or—oh!" Elodie jumped back and clapped her hands. "Where are my manners? I'm sure you're exhausted from your journey! And hungry! Do you want anything to eat or drink?"

"Oh, that would be wonderful, if you don't mind," I said as I lowered myself into a chair.

Elodie twirled around to face Marietta. "Could you be a dear and get us some tea and cookies, love?"

Marietta bowed her head, then strode into the kitchen without another word.

Elodie's smile vanished for a moment. "Don't mind her. She is still adjusting, I think. I don't know. She doesn't talk to me enough about it...and I don't feel comfortable inquiring. Every time I ask, she keeps saying, 'I'm fine, Elodie, my dear. A lot is on my mind.' I think there is something wrong, but I can't figure it out. I don't think she's seeing anyone else, but I may be mistaken." Elodie leaned forward, whispering, "We could find out together! Play a game of elusive spies, like we used to! Remember the stories Daddy used to tell? They were—" She shook her head. "Well, never mind those."

"You mean the one about the two spies that sailed from Janis to spy on the King of Perennes?" I asked, readying myself for the tale. "Yes, that was always my favorite. How did it go again?"

"Nanette..."

"Didn't it start with the old man telling his daughter he had riches abroad? I always loved that—"

"Doris Nanette!" Elodie rose. "Stop!"

I stared at her. "What? What's wrong?"

"Stop with the stories. They're not good for anyone."

"What do you mean? Daddy always told stories!"

"Yes, but that was then. Now..." Elodie frowned. "Now we're in Rosada."

"So?"

"Nanette, don't you know? Rosada outlawed stories."

THREE

. . . --

A few weeks passed before I truly settled into Rosada. The city harbored an unfamiliarity that wasn't common in Stilette. People didn't gossip, read fiction, or discuss the latest entertainment. No one smiled. Everyone walked with their heads down, eyes cast to the shadow, worried that someone watched their every movement. Elodie navigated it all, completely unalarmed. She continued chatting, keeping straight with the facts, and spent most of her days venturing into the city to shop for the latest goodies. I never doubted her ability to blend in with the highlife, loving every moment, completely and utterly oblivious to the world around her.

When she wasn't out, she sat by the window, reading one of the many law journals she had kept from her years of studying. Elodie had a knack for remembering little things, such as the details of an outfit to a specific case proposed in the Senate years before we were born. Why she never became an advocate eluded me, but I didn't question it. She made a life for herself in the city.

Yet, as she dove into the frivolities of the city, I watched her own spouse wither away. Marietta rarely spoke, a harshness in her gaze. Long after Elodie headed to bed each night with a newspaper or journal in hand, I often heard Marietta lock herself in a bathroom upstairs for an hour to complete her nighttime routine. One evening, after a night out with Elodie, Marietta arrived home in a futz as she forced me out of the washroom and locked herself inside without a word. It was as if she had to complete this routine to feel whole again. But she never talked about it.

But, despite the clear signs of Marietta's desire for more, I don't think Elodie noticed. She wrapped herself instead in *things*, arriving home each day with bags full of new clothes, tchotchkes, jewelry, and doodads. Neither Marietta nor I ever said a word as she placed a new vase on the table, purchased a new bookshelf, or hung a pristine set of curtains. These things made her happy.

They didn't harm anyone either.

For those first few weeks, I ignored Elodie's behavior. At least until she roped me into a scheme to refurbish *my* wardrobe like a game she would drag me into as a child.

It happened one fine morning when she waltzed into my bedroom and pulled out my green dress. "Nanette!" She said, scowling. After weeks of practice, she almost never called me Doris, thankfully. "This is absolutely appalling! What happened to all those beautiful dresses Mama made for you? This is repulsive, darling! How do you intend to find a suitor?"

I glanced at my wardrobe. I'd only traveled to Rosada with the simplest garments, selling the others for my voyage or leaving them behind as a donation. Gisela had kept a few of them as a parting gift, but I didn't mind my otherwise drab wardrobe.

Elodie had none of that, continuing with her rant, "Or, even if you aren't looking for marriage, you at least need something nice if you want a job! Even a tavern wench wears a bodice!"

That much was true. I'd been freeloading off my sister for a few weeks now. Even in their wealth, they could only support me for so long.

I guess expanding my wardrobe wasn't the *worst* idea imaginable.

Elodie hailed a cabby the next day. To my utter joy, Ryon Barnes pulled up, this time with a brown mare at the helm of his buggy. I hadn't taken a buggy since I arrived in Rosada, spending most of my time out and about walking to different destinations. Sure, I searched for him among the crowds, but I never saw his incandescent hair or wide smile. Now, as he pulled up against the smog-covered shadow of the city, his hair continued to glow like fire. His lips burst into a smile as soon as he saw me, his face as red as a cherry.

"Hello '*I'm a barn*,'" I called to him.

"And hello to you, Nanette the Sunset!" He jeered.

Elodie raised her eyebrows at me. "You two have met?"

"Mr. Barnes gave me a ride from the city on my first day here," I admitted.

"Oh. Lovely." Elodie grumbled as she climbed into the buggy.

I couldn't keep my smile back as I slid in next to her. Ryon winked at me, then, with a "hi-yah," sent his horse trotting towards the city center.

The ride proved one ultimate truth: Ryon Barnes was the only one who could out-talk Elodie. He babbled the whole way, pointing out different buildings and landmarks to me as the unofficial tour guide of the Capitol. Only did he pause when Elodie spoke over him to point out the fanciest shops or some poor government sap she knew from Marietta's work. I nodded to each of her remarks before returning to Ryon's exposition on the architecture and history of the city. He stopped himself short of telling any legends or rumors, sticking only with the facts.

Or, as he called them, state-sanctioned stories.

Ryon pulled up in the main plaza as he finished his last collection of "facts." He offered me a hand as I climbed out of the buggy, turning a bright red as I thanked him. It was honestly quite adorable.

But, wrapped up in his own embarrassment, once Elodie paid the fare, he sped off without even saying goodbye.

"Rude," Elodie muttered, "That gosh darn Ryon Barnes is so annoying, I swear on Daddy's grave..."

"Elodie!" I exclaimed. "Why would you say that? He seems nice."

"He doesn't shut up! Stories this, history that! He'll end up arrested... and the last thing I want is to be ON his buggy when that happens."

Didn't she realize how much she babbled on and on throughout the day? I suppose if she didn't hear her own voice, then the other person spoke way too much.

I didn't dare say that to her, though.

Elodie shook her head, then clapped her hands together in excitement, "Nevermind all this! Let's go find you some nice clothing!"

She yanked me through the plaza. It bustled with life, where two towering fixtures glared down at us. On one side stood the Capitol's Temple. Its Year Glass watched over the plaza, holding everyone in its silver gaze. I was never religious, but its watchful stare tugged at my curiosity, and I yearned to just step inside to marvel at the structure's beauty. I'm sure the stories within its walls were ones to behold! Perhaps one day I could go with Ryon...

I shook off the thought, following Elodie to the other side of the plaza where the Gallery waited with open arms. Its stained glass roof sent a cascade of colors over an array of shops and vendors. Yet, my mind kept going back to Ryon. What stories could he tell us about this beautiful city center? Why did I care? I met him only twice now! What did I know about him besides that he loved history, babbled endlessly, and was...well, quite attractive?

But then again, how soon had my heart fallen into Gisela and Yeshua's embrace? They helped me into this new world.

Though, even all my interactions with Gisela and Yeshua couldn't have prepared me for the thick crowds swarming the Gallery. People buzzed about like wasps, talking rapidly, their eyes wide with wonder. Elodie fit right in with the mix. I swore she knew everyone!

As we stopped at each vendor, she introduced me as her "feeble and humble sister."

"The poor dear owns nothing! Look at this dress...it's all she has!" Elodie lied to one shopkeeper.

I scoffed at her remarks, but after a few moments of negotiation, I realized the genius of her plight. The shopkeepers pitied me. The moment Elodie detailed my ever so terrible voyage from Volfium on the back of a smelly caravan, the shopkeepers gave me the best sales. Elodie jumped on each offer, not even asking for my opinion. She chose outfits garnished with bows, jewels, sparkles, and pearls. They dazzled with a rainbow of colors reserved for the wealthiest individuals. As I tried each one on, I felt out of place, only finding solace in a simple blue dress and a silver belt. Elodie declared that one too simple, but I held my ground.

After a day of shopping, I wanted at least one wearable outfit.

Elodie didn't understand why I liked that outfit. Why live in the Capitol if I did not want glamor?

Yet I only wondered... why live in the Capitol at all?

Ryon didn't give us a ride home that day. Elodie waved down an older cabby with an overweight horse. The cabby didn't speak the entire ride, giving Elodie the freedom to dominate the conversation... per usual.

She rambled about nonsense like when we were children. Elodie always fixated on the smallest details: how someone looked, a random newspaper article, or just how she needed to clean her nails. I loved hearing people talk, and I wanted to learn...but I did not care what a woman named Claudia wore to the Temple last week!

But these things made Elodie happy, so I never told her to be quiet.

I listened with more interest as she enthused about Marietta. She spoke with adoration for her spouse, going on about how smart and kind she was when they first met. Yet, she also worried about her sudden distant personality.

"Maybe she doesn't love me anymore, Nanette! Maybe she sees me as a failure. I never became an advocate. She must be sick of me and found herself a successful, pretty woman!"

"I doubt that. She is undergoing a big change, isn't she?" I asked.

"I suppose so. But I can't help but feel...distant from her if you understand what I mean?

"I'm sure she still loves you."

Even though it was but a small solace, it was enough to stitch happiness into her face.

When we arrived home, Elodie looped her arm around Marietta and led her into the bedroom, babbling away. Marietta smiled, but there remained that same glistening sadness in her eyes.

I didn't dwell on it. Instead, I retreated into my room and lay my new garments out on the bed. I had no intention of wearing at least half of these outfits. Most of them were far too itchy, frilly, and grand. Sure, they were lovely... but they weren't me.

Once the house turned dark, I carried the clothes downstairs, intending to deposit them into the washbasin with the rest of Elodie's clothes. Knowing my sister, she wouldn't even bat an eye when she folded them the next day. The outfits might have been slightly too big for her, but I never took Elodie to be the observant type. I kept the few dresses that weren't as grand to please Elodie, but I had every intention to phase these outfits as well.

Except for that blue dress—the one I adored.

As I opened the door to the kitchen, I slammed right into Marietta as she twirled out of the parlor in a long lacy skirt.

We stared at each other.

Then, I handed her my pile of clothes and asked, "Do you want these?"

Marietta's eyes widened.

As Marietta gathered the clothes from me, I ventured down into the basement to retrieve a bottle of brandy. I took a moment to run my fingers against the even golden stripes decorating the side of the cabinet before rushing back upstairs. In the parlor, I poured two glasses, and Marietta confided in me.

"I apologize that I haven't been very welcoming since you arrived. My transition has been hard," Marietta told me as she took a glass of brandy. "Most people are so accepting of it, but there is a fear that someone might not approve of my new reality. I didn't know you, so I kept my distance."

I can't say I really understood her fears, but I never considered her anything less than family. Father taught Elodie and me to never be critical or judgmental of one's path. Some people take longer to find themselves in this crazy world. We should all accept that and help if we can.

I always held that belief close to my chest.

I took her hand. "You're my sister now. The moment you married Elodie, you became my sister."

"Your sister," Marietta whispered. She smiled and recited it again, then cradled the new clothes I gave her close. "Thank you. You don't know how much it means to me."

"It's nothing."

"No. All of this. Your acceptance...the clothes...all of it is one step closer to feeling like I'm accepted." Marietta glanced at her feet, "I haven't wanted to trouble Elodie much with all the frivolities. She's been so wrapped up in your arrival."

"Elodie would love to take you shopping," I promised. If I knew anything about my sister, I knew that Elodie might have been a ditzy young woman, but she always had an open heart.

Plus, she did love a good shopping spree.

And without a doubt, she would adore finding Marietta a new wardrobe.

I said all of this, watching as Marietta searched my eyes. I can't imagine the thoughts in her head.

That's not my story to tell.

After we finished our cups of tea, well late into the night, she gathered the clothes into her arms and said, "Thank you, Nanette, I have a lot to consider."

"You're welcome." I rose with her, then paused. "Tell Elodie you want to go shopping tomorrow. You're not alone anymore, Marietta."

"And neither are you, Nanette. I'm glad to have you as my sister."

FOUR

. . . . −

Elodie welcomed Marietta's desire to redo her wardrobe with the excitement of a newlywed. She took Marietta in her arms and kissed her. With the newfound acceptance and outfits, Marietta changed as well; the color in her face flourished, less reserved while matching Elodie's constant energy. Well, maybe "matching" is a poor choice of words... but Marietta kept pace with my sister. From what Elodie told me one day over breakfast, this was the Marietta she fell in love with four years ago: the smiling, laughing individual who loved to dance.

I welcomed this newfound distraction. Elodie occupied herself with Marietta, leaving me to my own ways. So, while they shopped and laughed, I focused my energy on finding a job.

Yet I soon discovered that few places desired a nineteen-year-old immigrant from Volfium.

After multiple failed searches, Marietta came to my rescue.

Ever since Marietta confided in me, I'd traveled with her into town twice a week to visit the apothecary so she could collect a transitioning potion and some vitamins for Elodie. Located at the far east side of the Capital, where the walls bordered the graying mountain range, the shop sat undisturbed. No one paid much heed to it, and Marietta and I often entered as the only customers. The apothecary, an old fellow with poor eyesight, always greeted us with a smile.

Yet, I felt my own smiles begin to falter as my job search proved fruitless.

"Are you doing okay, Nanette? You haven't said much today," Marietta said as she collected her vials from the apothecary's counter.

"Oh, it's nothing really. Job hunting has been more difficult than I thought."

"Ah, yes. There's some hesitancy around outsiders. I might be able to help, though. Give me a couple days."

I didn't expect Marietta to find me anything, but a few days later, she came home with a grin spread from ear to ear. She discovered a listing at the Capitol Building for a scribe position for Captain Oberland, a senior captain in the Rosadian Guard responsible for watching over the Fifty-Eighth Division in the Capitol. This division left blood in their wake, responsible for ridding the streets of criminals and vagrants. Civilians never dared look those guards in the eye.

Despite the dark nature of his work, Captain Oberland was a jolly old fellow. He had a crooked foot that always dragged on one side, while his pointed mustache and goatee made his smile more pronounced. Whenever he laughed, it echoed down the hall.

Yet Captain Oberland couldn't read, write, or send telegraphs.

Hence the need for a scribe.

The captain hired me on the spot, marveling over my fluency and penmanship in both Rosadian and Volfi, as well as my ability with tap-code.

Yet, a scribe's job is nowhere near as jovial. Captain Oberland rambled, talking in circles, switching between events, and often missing key details. It made little sense: he spoke of individuals committing petty acts of thievery, only to shift the statement to say high crimes. Other times, he spoke of fights in alleys, backtracking to mention magic. None of it ever really lined up, making my work even more difficult. Despite how he always said, "Don't worry, Miss Ivans. You can finish tomorrow," I often worked late into the evening to get the notes right.

His telegraphs were even more confusing. When one came in, usually it comprised a string of letters and numbers.

...- —.-.

"VQE..." appeared often, and whenever I recited it to the captain, he would merely nod and continue with his day.

I couldn't figure out what it meant.

Marietta and I left every morning together to head to work. She took her time announcing her transition to her coworkers, slowly adding details to her outfits, or wearing her hair a different way. But even those slight changes created a noticeable improvement in her mood, and as we rode into town each morning, she babbled away about current events, work, and Elodie.

I enjoyed Marietta's company. At first, we ate lunch together every day. As Marietta focused more on her transition, she used her lunch hours to visit the apothecary on a regular basis, leaving me to eat at my desk or on the Capitol steps. As Marietta's focus turned more on her personal pursuits, I only saw her in the mornings. I often returned home after she did, and by the time I arrived, Marietta stood locked in Elodie's talkative grasp. So, with a pleasant smile, I bid them each goodnight, venturing into the kitchen to eat dinner before heading to bed.

For those first few weeks, my days ran like clockwork. I traveled to work with Marietta, listed to Captain Oberland ramble, sent telegraphs, and conducted filing. At dusk, I walked home alone, taking in the sights and breathing in a moment of silence. While the routine was pleasant enough, I wanted more. I daydreamed about Yeshua and Gisela. They were only a story at this point; I hardly remembered their faces, just the way they made my heart spin. It might not have been love—no, it was definitely lust—but it made me *feel something* more. I attempted to pleasure myself at night in a steam-filled bathtub, but it didn't fill the empty void.

Despite everything, really, I was alone.

I buried myself deeper into my work, staying late each night to finish Captain Oberland's reports. Yes, I tried to become friendly with the other scribes, but with no one telling stories, it was more like talking to ghosts.

Each day, I tried to arrive home by sundown to quell Elodie's nerves, but a day came where I lost track of time. I exited my windowless office to greet a moonless sky coated in a thick fog, reminiscent of Death's Grip back in Stilette. It suffocated the sky, so thick I couldn't see in front of me. Shadows beyond the gold-encrusted gas lamp haunted the path. My stomach churned. What demons lurked in the darkness tonight?

I hailed a cabby. A few shadows trotted by without noticing me before one finally pulled up, led by a disinterested brown horse.

None other than Ryon Barnes held the reigns.

"Nanette... out after sunset! Hello!" He waved.

"'*I'm a barn,*' what a surprise!" I chided.

"Gosh, I regret making that joke." He laughed. "It's been a few weeks, hasn't it?"

"Yes. And I am afraid I need a ride home today."

"Very well, hop on in!"

Giddy, I jumped into the back of his buggy.

Ryon grinned at me as he tugged at his horse's reigns. He continued to speak while navigating his horse through the fog. "I kept stopping by Ms. Lieu's, but she never wanted a ride. Really, I hoped to see you, but...well, you weren't there."

"I've been working."

"Oh! That's wonderful. Where?"

"The Capitol. I work as a scribe."

"Oh..." His voice hardened. "So you're writing history?"

"I write what Captain Oberland says is history, yes."

A brief silence, coupled with the horse's trotting, rested in the air. It didn't budge until the Capitol Building disappeared behind us.

Ryon whispered, "Do you believe everything that you write?"

I glanced at Ryon. His shoulders remained tense. Did I believe what I wrote? Most of the time, I paid little attention to Captain Oberland, sticking to my duty. Nothing more.

"I'm not sure," I replied. "Captain Oberland never seems set on one truth or another... he backtracks a lot and just... rambles."

"Sounds like he's flying off the ramble."

"Flying off the ramble?"

"Cause he's rambling... instead of the saying 'flying off the handle?'" His voice broke with embarrassment.

I giggled, "You're a silly man, 'I'm a barn.'"

He shrugged and said nothing else.

The silence fell again. Did I say something wrong? I

Ryon didn't let the air remain stale, slicing it open with a single question. "Why do you work for *them*?"

I fidgeted, glancing over my shoulder at the disappearing Capitol Building in the fog. "I need the money. People are hesitant to hire some immigrant from Volfium."

"Hm."

My head hurt. Was he suddenly judgmental of me? Did he hate me for what I said? Was I as bad as the guards?

Why did it matter what Ryon Barnes thought? I barely knew him.

But I liked him, as a friend at least, and he was one of the friendliest faces I'd met in Rosada.

I responded in haste. "I don't want to work there forever! But I don't know what to do yet. Please don't hate me. Please...it was hard to find work with my skill set..."

Ryon stopped his buggy and looked back at me. His hazel eyes locked with mine, and my stomach somersaulted, catching the bile rising in my throat.

"Why would you think I'd hate you?"

"Because I'm writing stories—"

"I might've gotten a bit grumpy there for a moment, but it's not your fault. You're performing a job like some cog in a machine...easy to replace with another. You're trying to survive like the rest of us." He glanced back at me and then towards the shadow of the Capitol Building. "It's a shame that these stories are history, and true history is a story. That's why they're illegal, y'know. They think we'll rebel. Like the Capitol Building? They say long ago that the Sister Queens of Rosada built it. But they didn't build it! They stole it in some war! But the government will push that away like a story and arrest whoever speaks such slanders." Ryon's face paled. "And you're a government worker... shit. You won't turn me in, right Nanette?"

I shook my head. "Why would I? In Volfium, we tell stories all the time. I miss them. They give life to everything."

Color returned to his cheeks as he smiled. "I knew I liked you! Why don't you sit up front with me? I got a bunch more 'stories' I can tell!"

Like my heart thumping, I hopped up onto the front bench with him. Our arms grazed each other. The hair on my arm rose.

We took the long way home. Ryon talked the entire way, pointing out different historical landmarks before whispering the true history behind them. As he spoke, I drowned myself in his presence. He sounded like roaring thunder. His presence felt like a forest, but he smelled of farmland. It brought back memories of my time with the caravan. Yeshua, Gisela, and I snuck into a barn and lay in the straw, waiting for the storm to pass over the nearby forest.

But when I recalled the memory, I pictured Ryon.

The moon hovered over the trees as Ryon pulled up in front of Elodie's home. Ryon helped me out of his buggy. We gazed at each other for a moment. I licked my lips, glancing at his mouth for a moment, then down at my feet. I didn't want to act on this sensation yet. This longing felt different from my time with Yeshua and Gisela. I wanted it to last. I yearned for it to stay.

Instead, I gave him a single statement. "I'll be working late for quite a while and will need a ride most days."

His eyes brightened. "I can schedule you in every day around this time if you'd like."

"I would like that."

Despite Ryon's objection, I paid him a single gold coin before waving goodbye. I watched him lead his horse away until finally, the mist swallowed him home.

My heart rode on a cloud as I entered the home. I couldn't say I was in love, but I certainly fancied Ryon. The way he smiled warmed my heart, his voice soothed my ears, and his eyes garnered my attention.

I ignored Elodie as she shrieked over my tardiness and only grazed across my plate before heading upstairs. Nothing else mattered. I was in a cloud of happiness! And it waltzed with me up the stairs and into the bathroom, where I sank into the tub and mingled with my fantasies well into the night.

FIVE

•••••

For the next few weeks, no matter my workload, I waited for Ryon to pull up outside the Capitol Building rather than walking home. We always took the long way back to the house, and each time, despite his insistence that there was no need, I paid him a gold coin. At first, we kept the conversations civil, debating about half histories and truths in Rosada, discussing stories and rumored magic, and conversing about what Captain Oberland had me write. Sometimes, Ryon's innate curiosity persuaded me to tell him everything, even things belonging to government eyes only. But he was right. So much of it was preposterous.

I was the first to open about my personal life. As a thick mist wove its way through the city one day, I told Ryon how my father died during Death's Grip.

"What's Death's Grip?" He asked.

"I suppose you don't have it here. In Volfium, it's when the fog grows so thick, you can hardly see it. They say that is when Death comes to release the souls into oblivion." I held my hand out in front of me to catch the fog, "I hope that means Papa is at peace."

"Were you close with your father?"

"Very." I told him about how my father used to tell stories, venturing to the local tavern where his tales would come to life. Papa educated Elodie and me, taking us to the different taverns in the cities to learn about others, and hear their tales. Ryon listened eagerly, his eyes wide with interest.

I suppose Stilette seemed like a fantasy to him.

"My father's the one who taught me tap-code... for the telegraphs," I added. Tap-code, overall, was a rare skill set. Most people still resorted to the old pen and paper.

"You know tap-code?" Ryon gawked. "That's amazing! I always wanted to learn."

"I can teach you."

His face cracked in two with a smile.

The next few days, I taught him the tap-code alphabet, giggling as I produced the shrill beeping noises of the taps.

.-. -.— —- -.

"Ryon." I said, "That's how you say your name."

"That sounds attractive." He repeated the noise. "And what about you?"

-. .- -. . - - .

"That's it," I whispered.

He recited it slower, "Beautiful..."

Despite our camaraderie, Ryon didn't tell me much about his personal life at first. He focused more on babbling about different buildings and histories or learning tap-code... or about me.

Until a few days later, when Ryon arrived thirty minutes late for our rendezvous. He apologized, flustered, and we rode in silence.

I pried, "Ryon? What's bothering you?"

He glanced at me. "Oh, don't mind me. You don't need to hear about my messy life."

"I want to, though." I placed my hand on his warm, rough arm.

He stared at me for a moment, then slowed his white horse to a steady trot. He sighed, "Family problems. You know. Family is great until they decide things for you."

I nodded. My father never made my decisions directly, but he always held me to a certain standard. Then, of course, there was Elodie, who tried to dress me like a doll.

Ryon licked his lips and continued. "Money's been tight. I live on a farm a bit away from here with my ma, pa, and sisters in a two-room farmhouse. But Pa's frustrated I keep taking a horse each day to run, and I quote, 'a profitless business to woo the rich and make shit money.'" He gripped his reins tighter. "He wants me to work on the farm. Forget about this cabby business... cause he seems to think I'm out here mingling with a bunch of fat cats. But... I love coming into the city and doing this job! I get to talk to people and learn about history and see people and sights. And I love—" His eyes met mine, and his cheeks burned, "I love spending time with my patrons, like you. Not that I have a lot, but..." his voice trailed.

I squeezed his arm. "Well, I don't want you to go away. I look forward to this ride home every single day."

Ryon tensed beneath my grip, then shook his head, "Pa doesn't care, and unless I find a good reason or start making more coin, I'm gonna have to stop these joy rides. Pa says the cost of bringing a horse and buggy to the city isn't worth it when we could use it on the farm and everything. Plus, my medicine is getting more expensive and..."

I stopped him, "Medicine?"

He scowled, realizing what he said. "It's no big deal. I get blood-sugar issues. At least that's what the apothecary said when I was a kid. Need to do injections and such to keep myself from going into shock. Kinda pricey, though..."

I touched his arm. "And your dad thinks keeping you on the farm will...do what exactly?"

"Save us money. Think he wants to make sure I'm healthy, too, though. But I don't want to be my illness, you know? I'm more than that."

"Do you have any other skills so you can work in the city instead and become more independent?" I asked.

"Not really. I mean, yeah, I can write and read, but you gotta have connections to get a job with that. Can't do much manual labor." He shrugged, "The cabby job is good... There's just a lot of us, and locals have their favorite cabby. I'm not that with most people."

"You're my favorite cabby."

He flushed.

"But..." I pondered, "I guess we need to find you more patrons... or connections."

"Pa's about to go off like a pistol, I think. He won't let me take the horse much longer unless I bring in a handful of coins soon."

"Let's try, though. Please. I want to help."

"Alright...yeah. That would be nice."

We shared a smile.

For the rest of the trip, Ryon returned to his usual loquacious nature, talking about how a group of Guards vandalized a wall in a mountain town. He spoke with lust about the mountains, with awe about the plains, and with complete fascination about the sea. Nothing deterred his interest. If he knew how to tell a story, he would have been a marvelous storyteller.

But in a nation that prohibited storytelling, the talent belongs to a select few.

He pulled up in front of Elodie's house, and as always, helped me out of the buggy. For a moment, we stood in the yard in silence, staring at each other. Did his heart flutter like mine? What did he want from me?

Did he share the same desires?

Ryon scuffed his shoes against the grass and rubbed the back of his neck. "Well, um, have a good evening, Nanette. I suppose I will see you next time."

I grabbed his arm before he turned. "Wait."

He froze.

"Tomorrow, I have off. We could...meet up if you would like? We could discuss finding you customers or a job...make a plan, of sorts." Heat rose in my cheeks, but my stomach churned. What if he said no? Would I never see him again?

But he grinned at me and said, "I'd like that very much."

I waited on the porch, swaying back and forth in a dress Elodie forced upon me. Once she found out I had a *date*, Elodie fussed over my appearance, giddy as ever about the prospects that her little sister might finally come upon a suitor. With Marietta to tame her, we found a decent outfit. It highlighted my curves without being too promiscuous.

When Elodie asked me for my date's name, I lied with a commonplace name: John. Elodie had vocalized her distaste for Ryon on multiple occasions to me, often making a point to avoid his buggy. I am sure if she knew that Ryon and I were meeting, steam would have poured out of her ears.

As I stood on the porch for Ryon, with the late summer breeze stroking my hair, a thousand thoughts raced through my head. What if he didn't come? What if he was only being nice? What if he didn't *like* me like that?

But I'd seen the way he smiled. I wasn't totally aloof, right?

At exactly noon, Ryon rounded the bend on foot wearing a handsome brown suit. He trimmed his patchy beard, and his red curls lay matted back against his head. He raised a hand to greet me as I raced over to the edge of the property.

His face turned red. "Nanette, you look like a sunset."

"And you look pretty good for a barn."

"That's getting old." He rebuked.

"You love it."

He smiled.

I laced my arm through his arm, and in the most cordial fashion, we walked towards the city. He decided not to bring his buggy to avoid his father's anger, but I didn't mind. It gave us a chance to talk, to giggle, and to whisper stories. We didn't really talk about his job prospects much. Instead, we talked about minuscule things: our favorite foods, our hobbies, and just...our lives. He was a stunning man, really. He had this jovial nature not yet worn away by the city, and when he laughed, I swore the wind tried to steal it.

Ryon took me to a café in the heart of the Capitol, right along the perimeter of the Gallery. We ordered a couple lemon cakes and tea, then sat in awkward silence as we picked at our meal. It hit me like a storm. This was the date. Not the walking. Not the rides in his buggy. Here, at the café. Right now.

Eventually, Ryon looked up from his half-eaten cake, "You really are as stunning as a sunset."

I grinned to myself, then said, "Well, you're quite the looker yourself."

"I didn't expect you to be like this, though," Ryon said. "You're such a good listener and thoughtful. When I first met you and found out you were Ms. Lieu's sister, I was shocked! She's so—"

"Stubborn?"

"Yes, that's a good word for it." He laughed.

"She has always liked order and things and gossip. I think that's why she liked the Capitol. Our home, Stilette, isn't as orderly or pristine. We have magicians in the streets, storytellers—"

"In the sheets?"

"What?"

"Storytellers in the sheets, instead of the streets." He turned red, still smiling.

"Mr. Barnes! That's a lewd statement!" I kicked his ankle.

"Ow! Sorry!"

I stuck my tongue out at him.

"Sorry, really. Go on. Please," He leaned forward on his elbows, "I want to hear about your life in Stilette. It sounds wonderful."

"There's not much to say. It was a city on stilts, filled with smiles and performances... and stories. So many stories..." I trailed off, staring at the people walking past the café with their heads down and eyes solemn. "I miss the stories."

"You mean the ones not sanctioned by the government?"

"Exactly."

Ryon glanced around a few times, then leaned across the table, whispering, "They're not gone, Nanette. I can show you."

"Aren't we supposed to be job hunting?" I teased.

"Eh, we got time. C'mon. Lemme show you."

After we finished our meal, Ryon led me away from the Gallery, past the Temple, and into a network of dark alleys just out of the Guard's purview. I clenched his arm as my heartbeat rose.

He nudged me. "Relax. It's safe, okay?"

"Are you sure?"

"Just stay close to me."

I wasn't planning to let go, keeping my fingers laced around his arm like my life depended upon it. Where was he taking me? These alleys belonged to terrifying stories that kidnapped women and slaughtered men. But Ryon walked without fear, a bounce still in his step. Was he leading me somewhere to steal my heart and eat it? He could murder me right here and there. I should have listened to Elodie!

I shooed the paranoia away. Ryon wasn't capable of such evil! I shouldn't let such fear take me captive.

I dismissed it just in time. Ryon led me through the alleyways and between the bricks. He tapped once on a stone as we walked, similar to tap-code, and a gust of wind wrapped around me. Ryon led me around a bend in the path, and as if a cloak was removed from the path, before me stood droves of stalls, lining the walls in a sort of secret marketplace, bustling with life.

My fear left me with my dropping jaw, and awe took hold of my body and tugged me into the fray. Individuals shouted, passing goods around from all different rungs in society's ladder. The richest men, the poorest woman, and everyone in between occupied the street. No one noticed two newcomers, completely locked in their own secretive banter right beneath the Guard's eyes.

Magic. It had to be magic, acting as a protective barrier. How else could something like this thrive?

"Take a gander, Nanette. They're not here trading money for goods."

I glanced around the alley. He was right. No one exchanged coins. Instead, they exchanged words with such vigor and excitement it could only mean one thing: in exchange for goods and services, they performed tales, gossip, magic, and stories.

A yelp of excitement nearly escaped my lips. I covered my mouth and glanced at Ryon, unable to contain my smile. He beamed at me, his eyes sparkling with delight. Together, we walked among the patrons, keeping our ears open for different tales. I gathered each one in my heart. They filled the air: a story of a forest queen, another about a man who cast fire from his fingers, and one more a pirate crew lost at sea.

They were all fantastical in their own way.

Magical.

And real.

Just like the fire-breather performing tricks in the alley. Or the children who made coins disappear.

In exchange for each story, vendors gave potions and elixirs, magical tricks and acts, and unique goods and services. Each transaction was seamless, almost without question. Children played by the wall, listening to the stories, while their mothers vended the illegal goods. Even in such an unground market, light prevailed. People smiled. They laughed.

They were free to be human again.

I spun to face Ryon. "This is amazing! I never thought something like this could exist!"

"No one ever does. Imagine what we could do if stories and magic could come out of the shadows."

"The Guard wouldn't have a chance! Oh, Ryon...thank you for showing me this! It's fantastic!" I threw my arms around his neck and kissed his cheek.

He fidgeted, his face turning that adorable shade of red.

"Can we stay here for a while? I want to listen to more stories!" I begged.

"Of course! C'mon. There's this one old lady over here who I love listening to. C'mon!"

Ryon and I spent all day in the Black Market. We absorbed ourselves in the stories, watched the gossip, and inhaled the stench of life. Part of me wanted to stay there forever. But as the sun began its orange descent, the vendors packed, the magic dwindled, and the alley was nothing more than a strip of pavement once more.

Arm-in-arm, Ryon and I headed back down the road towards Elodie's home. We talked nonstop, recanting every story in whispers, laughing at the twists, and blushing with each flirtatious jab. Ryon argued the best story was the one about the talking llama, while I insisted it was the story about the Forest Queen. The whole conversation was natural.

Wonderful.

Perfect.

I didn't want the day to end.

Yet, inevitably, we arrived outside the gate to Elodie's home. Ryon and I stopped, our fingers touching, gazes locked.

Ryon broke it first, flabbergasted, "Today...it was nice."

"It was," I replied.

"We never looked for a job for me or anything."

"There's always tomorrow."

He fidgeted, "Yeah...I... yeah."

I waited a moment.

He continued, "Listen, I'm sorry. I know I act like a flirt and everything, but I haven't been with a girl before, so I don't really know what I'm supposed to do now. Because I want to kiss you, but I don't know if right now the time is, and I don't want to mess this up. It's just that I really like you, Nanette, but what if I scare you away or anything and—"

I stepped forward and laced my arms around him. He froze, mouth half ajar as I pressed my lips against his mouth.

He gaped for a second, then melted into the kiss. His mouth twirled over mine, desperate and hungry. It wasn't the same as when Yeshua and Gisela kissed me: polished, confident, and loveless. But with Ryon, the kiss was endless. Sloppy. Passionate. But true. Our lips crashed like two disoriented chickens without their heads, but the emotion reigned deep in my core.

We pulled apart, leaving only an inch between us, our breaths heavy.

"When can I see you again?" Ryon asked.

"Whenever you want..." I cooed before brushing my lips over his once again.

"Mm..." He sighed as he pulled away. "My father will kill me if I venture into the city tomorrow. But...I'll pick you up at our usual time the next day, okay?"

I nodded, "It's a date."

Our fingers separated, our bodies pulled back, and with one final glance over my shoulder, I headed into the house, humming to myself.

SIX

—••••

Elodie waited for me in the foyer. I waltzed right past her, not even noticing the way she gripped a book in her hands, knuckles turning white, while her green eyes blazed.

"Oh, hello Elodie!" I sang.

"Where have you been?" She snapped at me.

"I told you I had a date today!"

"I knew you had a date...but I never imagined it would be with Ryon Barnes of all people!"

"What does it matter if it was? I'm a grown woman!" I snapped.

"You don't *know* Mr. Barnes, Nanette. He's bad news!"

"I know plenty about him! What do you find so repulsive about him, anyway?"

"He just is!"

"Why?" I threw my arms in the air. "Is it because he talks a lot and listens more? Maybe if you were quiet for once, you might actually like what he has to say!"

"Are you even listening to what he's saying?" Elodie approached me with a scowl.

"Yes!"

"Doris—Nanette! He wants to overthrow the government! Whenever I see him, he just goes on and on about how terrible the Senate is and how everything is a lie! You work for the government; how would you feel attacked while you were working!?!"

"Well, he wouldn't! He doesn't even want the government to fall. He wants it to be honest... that's all!" I laughed, "You don't work there, Elodie. You just quit studying law to reap the benefits of Marietta's hard work!"

"I left law so I could enjoy myself, instead of wasting away in textbooks for years."

"And while you enjoy yourself, you don't see the truth!"

"What you're saying is treasonous."

"It's true. I write lies for Captain Oberland every day. I hate it! But I do it so I can earn some money and get out of this fucking house!"

Elodie gaped at me. I never spoke to her like this. Usually, I avoided confrontation and kept my true opinions under lock and key. But I really liked Ryon. A lot.

No. I was in love. That wonderful kiss solidified everything. Elodie would always be my sister, but she didn't know Ryon.

I wouldn't let her tarnish his name.

Finally, Elodie hissed, "What would Papa say?"

"About what?"

"All of this! The profanity, the treason, the... everything!"

"It's not treason to voice displeasure!" I scoffed. "Besides, how would you know what Papa would say? You left! You weren't there the past couple of years of his life! You didn't watch him die like I did!" I glared out the window, holding back my tears.

"How can you say that?" Elodie shouted. "I came here for a reason!"

"But you never returned!"

"It's not that simple!"

"Why not? This city is terrible! There are no stories. In fact, Papa would be proud of me for speaking up! He loved stories, Elodie! And now here you are, living in a city without a single song or tale." I wiped my eyes and whispered, "We used to love listening to stories. What ever happened to you, Elodie?"

"I learned the truth." Elodie straightened her back. So she was almost as tall as me.

"The truth?"

"Come with me to the Temple tomorrow. You'll learn as well."

Elodie woke me at the crack of dawn the next morning. I slumped after her into the buggy, waiting for us outside, glaring at the early morning mist. Exhaustion hung from my eyelids after a restless night. I spent half the time thinking about Ryon and his uneven smile and the other half tossing and turning over my argument with Elodie. Even as I got into the buggy, a tension remained.

"Nanette, this is Karl!" Elodie introduced me to the cabby as I climbed into the carriage. "He's a fine young man, isn't he?"

I responded with pleasantries but disregarded Elodie's clear attempt to pull me away from Ryon. She didn't understand. Even if Gisela and Yeshua arrived again tomorrow, tempting me with their hands and their kisses, I don't think I would have lain with them. I didn't dream of those nights anymore, nor did I regret them. Instead, my fantasies involved Ryon.

Elodie said little for once. I fidgeted with my fingers as the silence dominated the journey. It was odd. I'd grown accustomed to Ryon's babbling or Elodie's non-stop chatter. So, I turned my attention to the scenery. Everything reminded me of Ryon: the wind through my hair could have been his hands, and the sweat on my lips might have been a kiss.

But even more, I wanted to talk about him with Elodie. Growing up, I used to listen as she giggled about her suitors. I couldn't wait until I found love so she could share in the excitement!

Why couldn't she just be happy for me now?

The buggy stopped in the main plaza outside the Temple. It glistened above us, with patrons entering the pews in droves. Elodie grabbed my hand and led me towards the structure.

"I am so happy you agreed to come with me for morning prayer, Nanette!" Elodie babbled, keeping up the happy facade.

"I never thought of you as a religious type."

"It provided... comfort when I moved here all alone. You'll understand soon enough!"

I glowered at the building. While the first time I saw the building, a sense of awe overcame me. Now I only squirmed with mild disgust. In one of our long cab rides around the city, Ryon told me how the Order of the Effluvium evicted hundreds of individuals from their homes to build this Temple.

Or perhaps it was the morgue, where dreams and stories went to die.

My soul weighed heavily as I walked inside, behind Elodie.

Yes, the structure gleamed with endless rows of pews and dazzling stained glass. In the atrium above, an hourglass-shaped structure counted the passing moments with silver and red gems. All the patrons in their simple whites, beiges, and blues belonged to a watercolor painting. Perhaps if I hadn't learned the history, I might have gazed in awe, but like everyone else, I kept my head lowered.

I sat upon a bench with Elodie. A man dressed in a garnet robe walked along the aisles, with two women trailing behind him in blue and green robes. They bore a smaller version of the glass fixture above on their chests, humming hymns as they walked down the aisle.

The man in the garnet robe took the spot by the podium.

"That's Elder Vic Tor Cordova," Elodie whispered. "His family has been part of the Order of the Effluvium for centuries. That's his nephew, Donovan." Elodie pointed to a child trailing behind the two robed women. The child wore gold and kept his head high, bright blue eyes steady on his face. "He's already a prodigy of the Order, so they say. His father is in the Guard."

"Great story…" I mumbled. Elodie didn't hear me, her own interest completely locked on Elder Vic Tor.

The Elder raised his hands to the sky. I don't remember the prayer he said word for word. I didn't want to remember. Even if I did, I would never want to repeat such lies. It left me feeling sick to my stomach. He spoke about how we had to be purified for the Effluvium's sake, keep magic from polluting the air, and to slaughter our dependency on lies and stories. Facts were facts, history was true, and anything else was slander. With each story, a demon would come.

I gagged as he finished his prayer. No wonder the government behaved with such distaste. The Order of the Effluvium pocketed these ideas, cradled them, then sent them out into the world. Elder Vic Tor charmed the audience, his smile and song soft. His nephew swayed to the similar beat, using his innocence to persuade people to climb into the crevasses beneath the building for something called a "cleanse."

My head spun throughout the service. Every word sounded like a plague, every line tasted like rot, and every hymn smelled like death. It called for order. For purity.

For being cleansed.

No wonder Elodie fell in love with the Order's teaching. Elder Vic Tor filled a void left behind by my father. He spoke with the same tenderness, but while my father preached acceptance and creativity, Elder Vic Tor demanded obedience and order.

As soon as the service ended, I raced out of the Temple and heaved in the alleyway. Elodie chased after me, "Nanette!?! What's wrong?"

"How can you listen to that?" I cried.

"I know, their teachings are overwhelming and heartbreaking at first—"

"Their teachings say that Papa is in Hell!" I screamed at her. "It doesn't make sense! Stories and gossip... they're what we thrive on in Stilette! Isn't religion built on stories? Isn't it... a story?" I washed my eyes. "I don't like this. Always thought this city was wrong... I felt it the moment I arrived. This doesn't make any sense..."

"Doris—Nanette, Nanette... relax. I felt the same way originally," Elodie squeezed my hands. "But the Order provides, well," she giggled, "order! Notice how there is no vile scum in the streets or magicians creating strange explosions? How many times did the small village north of Stilette get burned down by a misplaced magician? Come now, Nanette. Can you not see the peace here?"

I glared at Elodie. "Then where are all the homeless and poor?"

"There just aren't any. Can you not accept the possibility that the Order helped create a utopia?"

"It's not a utopia."

"I wouldn't choose to stay here if it weren't. I only want the best for my child."

"Child?" I cocked my head to the side and asked, "What are you talking about?"

"Nanette... I'm pregnant!"

On the ride back, Elodie told me all the details. Her monthly bleeds stopped about three months ago, right before I arrived from Stilette. She had been trying for a baby for quite some time, which prevented her from journeying back home following Father's death. It reduced our tension; at least to an extent, I understood the "why" to her behavior.

Even if I still disapproved of it.

Marietta, Elodie, and I celebrated that evening as a family. Marietta had me bring up a bottle of wine from the basement, and we uncorked it with a celebratory cheer. While I rejoiced in their laughter and smiles, by the time night fell, my world had spiraled into headaches and fear. I didn't spend my evening daydreaming about Ryon. Instead, I tossed and turned all night, recalling the terror caused by the Order.

A hollowness followed me out of bed and downstairs the next morning. Marietta noticed it as we rode into work.

"Nanette, what's wrong?" She asked, adjusting her curls as she spoke.

I chose each word with care. "I... cannot help but wonder if Captain Oberland speaks the truth. Do you believe everything that the Order and government says? I want to believe them, but it is hard... especially for a foreigner like myself."

Marietta stared ahead for a moment. She sighed. "I believe there are half-truths spoken by a select few. I try not to be one of those people. It's hard, though. When a commander tells you to fight, you fight. Or in my case, when the Head of the Treasury tells you to move funds or balance the books, you cannot deny it."

"So...no?"

Marietta shrugged.

"Then why work for them?"

"Sometimes, we have to do what we don't agree with to survive."

Wasn't that what I told Ryon?

I don't know if I believed it anymore.

Marietta and I didn't speak for the rest of the trip. My own thoughts wandered as I climbed up the Capitol stairs and wandered into my office. Captain Oberland waited for me, his feet up on his desk, a wide smile on his lips, "Ah, Doris. Good, good. I've been waiting for you. Lots to report. Yes. Lots."

"Good morning, Captain. Give me a moment." I gathered my notepad and pencil to begin his daily transcription.

Usually, I would zone out, writing each word without a second thought. For the first time that day, I really paid attention to what Captain Oberland said. He always rambled and concocted half-truths in his reports... but until then, I never quite *listened*.

"So, we fended off two—twenty men in the street with gun powder. They did—they fought back relentlessly. And all because they... um... that's right! They used magic to vandalize a building! The street will never look the same! What a shame! We caught and killed two of them. What a battle! Right here in the Capitol! Ha!" Captain Oberland exclaimed.

As I wrote each word, I picked up on the way he circled around, creating a redeemable history out of small veracious pieces. Each reason came with a revelation, a defense, or a sudden "aha!"

I grew frustrated as he spoke, though. As he finished the story of the supposed twenty men, my fingers slipped. The ink scrolled across the page as my hands unconsciously directed the next phrase: *We killed two men for no wrongdoing.*

I stared at the words and raised my pen, ready to cross them out. But that was the truth... wasn't it? There were probably only two men. Perhaps they were using a bit of magic to enjoy a night. I doubted there was any vandalism, and there was no fight. No battle. Only two innocent men... killed.

"Did you get that down, Doris?" Captain Oberland pried.

"Yes, yes, of course." I punctuated the statement and handed it to the captain. I held my breath as he glanced over at my work. The captain couldn't read, but it didn't prevent my heart from racing. What if he was lying, and he learned how to read?

But seconds later, he scribbled his standard signature at the bottom of the statement, then handed it back to me for filing.

I got away with it.

Sweat gathered on my palms as my head pounded. My stomach somersaulted despite my success. How many lies did the government feed us? How many state-sanctioned histories sat in these walls?

Had anyone else tried to rewrite history like this?

I couldn't focus throughout the rest of the day, missing telegraphs as they came in or constantly dropping files on the ground. By the time lunch rolled around, sweat drenched me from head to toe. Captain Oberland, convinced I had come down with a stomach bug, sent me home for the day without fanfare.

Rather than going home, I meandered in circles around the city to search for Ryon. Where could he be? What if he was one of those two men murdered? Had he been out celebrating our kiss or chattering away with one of his friends? Why hadn't I seen his buggy?

My mind raced with every possibility. What if they captured him? What if he was sick? What if his father told him not to return to the city anymore?

Ryon's voice pulled me from my panic. "Nanette!?!"

I found him sitting on the edge of a fountain eating lunch with a few other cabbies.

He dropped his sandwich and raced over to me. "What's wrong? You look terrible!"

"I did it," I croaked.

"Did what?"

"I changed history."

SEVEN

- -...

Ryon held me close in his buggy while I told him every-thing that had happened over the last couple of days. He stroked my hair, rocked me, and listened to every word without interruption. Sure, Ryon had a reputation for babbling, but he also knew how to listen. He hung onto every one of my words. Instead of a half comforting statement like "It'll be okay" or "It's fine, relax," Ryon instead cupped my face and whispered, "I understand."

"Why do they do this?" I asked.

"To control us. To make people like your sister think the world is okay."

"Elodie would say you're manipulating me. But you aren't." I wiped my eyes. "You can't be."

"I clearly wooed you with my punderful jokes." He grinned.

I rolled my eyes.

"But, really..." Ryon grimaced as he spoke, "When we met, you had this type of spark in you. You're the one who pointed out how people don't smile. You noticed how many guards were around. It was all you."

That was true.

"I didn't force you to believe anything I said. You could have easily thought I was some loon making up stories and discarded me."

That was also true.

"But you didn't. You listened, you argued, and you formed your own opinions. I never told you to change what Captain Oberland said, right? Really hope I didn't because... I want this to be your rebellion. We each have our own battles to fight." Ryon cracked a smile. "Besides, I think you have more the tenacity to manipulate me. You dazzled me like a sunset, after all."

Ryon Barnes, I swear, he always knew what to say. He rambled often, but somehow his words always came together seamlessly.

I responded with a kiss. A deep kiss. A passionate one. After a few moments, we pulled apart, blushing and laughing.

But the mood changed as I stared past him at the stone structures. The city beckoned; the city roared; the city lied.

"I want to learn the truth behind this city. The true history. Not some... state-sanctioned lie." I met his gaze, "Please."

"Do you really?" Ryon asked with a sobering glance.

"Yes. I do. My whole life, someone else always showed me the world. I saw Stilette through my father, the countryside through Gisela and Yeshua, and now I'm seeing the Capitol through you and Elodie. But I don't want that. I want to see everything, hear everything, and make my own decisions. Please. Can't you help me?"

He glanced down the road, then towards the towering Temple down the road, before turning back to me. "I can show you things, Nan. Terrible things that you can't imagine. Things you would be better off not knowing. Most people have never seen them... and... it's heartbreaking. I would hate to make you cry."

"Show me." My confidence didn't waver. But inside, I trembled. What could Ryon be showing me that turned his usual sunny demeanor gray?

Ryon directed the buggy away from the city with his aloof black horse. It was a slow, steady ride, navigating from the well-structured roads of the city into the dismantled cobblestone of the outskirts and onto the dirt road by the farmlands. Around each bend, it was like entering a new world. The well-to-do lived with luxury, but those without much lived in squalor. Ryon didn't comment on it. His face pulled in a frown, his hand on my arm, only breaking the staid façade to pay me a glance.

We passed by the sparse shrubs, through the fields of grains, and mooing cattle. Ryon brought his horse to a slow trot just outside a farmhouse.

"Welcome to my home..." Ryon said to me, his smile returning for one moment.

"I thought you lived in a barn, Mr. Barnes," I quipped.

"Only when I don't wanna deal with my parents." He winked.

"Wait..." My face reddened. "Am I here to meet your parents?"

"Nah, gotta show you something up the road from here. Figured I'd drop off the horse first... though..." He glanced at the house. "Ma's peeking out the window. I think you can't escape her even if you tried."

I cursed under my breath, "Fine."

Ryon led the horse over to the stalls. The other horses he often used for the buggy peaked out, and the brown one stomped its foot in excitement upon seeing me. I smiled at it before allowing Ryon to take my hand and lead me towards the farmhouse.

His mother greeted us in the doorway, "Ryon! You're home early! And who's your lady friend?"

"We're just passing through, Ma," Ryon muttered.

Ryon looked just like his mother, with a narrow nose and hazel eyes. Only his hair was different, and as I entered the home, I realized it was his father who blessed him with a head of flames. At the counter, his father stood peeling potatoes. He didn't look up from his work, brow furrowed, entirely focused.

Four younger girls bolted out of the backroom as we stepped inside the house. All four of them looked exactly like Ryon with ginger hair, a freckled face, and large smiles.

"Ryon's home early!" The youngest chanted.

His father didn't turn, saying, "You finally gonna stop going into the city then?"

"Honey, be nice!" Mrs. Barnes snapped at him. "He's brought home a lady friend! See!"

His father turned and raised his eyebrows. "Well, well, well. That clears up this lot plenty, then. Shoulda known you were seeing a lady!"

"Dad!" Ryon protested.

I came to his rescue, curtsying as I introduced myself. "I'm Doris Nanette Ivans. You can call me Nanette, though. It's wonderful to meet you."

Mrs. Barnes held out her hand, "What a pleasure—"

"I'm Queenie!" the youngest child interjected, then, with a flash of her finger, pointed at each of her sisters from shortest to tallest, "And that's Martha, and Gloria, and Wilma!"

I smiled, but a strange bout of envy wove through my stomach. Part of me yearned for a simpler time when the biggest argument I had with Elodie would be about who got the last of our mother's cookies.

The sisters bickered and giggled nonstop, tossing words between themselves, dominating the conversation in the room. While Ryon's father remained silent, his mother joined in the discussion, asking me many questions: When did Ryon and I meet? Where did I get that accent? What is it like in Stilette? What do I do for a living? The questions trailed one after the other. I could hardly keep up with their banter.

Ryon was unusually quiet with his family. I gripped his hand, squeezing it for reassurance as his mother served a meal of mashed potatoes, green beans, and bread. I restrained the urge to gag as I tried the mashed potatoes. The texture reminded me of vomit... but I held my tongue and ate around it.

As we finished our meal, Queenie piped up, looking me dead in the eyes, "Are you going to marry our brother?"

"Oh, um—"

Ryon leapt to his feet. "And we're going! Thanks for the meal, Ma, Pa... I'll see you later!"

I waved goodbye as Ryon rushed me out of the house, his face once again beet red. His little sisters followed us to the fence, giggling and waving. He didn't dare turn back.

Once we rounded the bend, I placed a hand on his chest, slowing his pace. "Are you alright?"

"Yes, sorry... they're excited, that's all." Ryon looked away from me. "I told you, I hadn't dated before. I'm almost twenty-one. I'm not married or anything. My father sees me as a disappointment."

"Why? You're making money. You're doing great things—"

"I'm a cabby making little-to-nothing."

"Yes, but—"

"He always wanted more for me." Ryon kicked the ground as we walked. "but Mom's just happy I'm alive. I told you... I've got a blood-sugar problem. So when I was a kid, I was really sick. Would get dizzy and lethargic. The local alchemist didn't think I'd live past twelve... and they couldn't figure out what was wrong with me, either. Nothing really worked. So, I didn't really play or do much of anything as a kid. My parents' home became my castle. One day I found a bunch of old books in the attic and dove into them. Guess that's why I started liking stories. Ma and Pa didn't even know they had them...so I hid them away and read by candlelight."

I smirked, picturing a young Ryon dripping wax on his bed from the candle, enthralled by the books.

"When I was about ten years old, my dad took me into the city to see a well-known apothecary. They gave me some injection that I still use today. I told you about that, right? Still don't know what it is, but it fixed whatever the problem was, and by the time I was fourteen, I was like anyone else." Ryon scowled for a moment. "But I didn't really get along with other kids once I was out in the world. All those jokes you find endearing, that's after years of people not getting them or thinking I'm 'odd.' People stayed away from me, thought I was in trouble. I started getting into some trouble here and there. Drank a bit, smoked some...but mostly, I talked about what I read in those books. Caught the attention of some...including my pa. He ransacked my room, found the books, and burned them all. It took a while for me to talk to him again."

I touched Ryon's arm as he continued prattling.

"I started behaving more as I got older. Stayed away from drinking much and smokes, tried to keep my mouth closed... but Pa and I never mended our relationship after that. Other people in town veered from me still. It's why I went to the Capitol for work...no one knows me there. But I guess...people just don't like me...so I never brought home a girl. And... sorry... I'm babbling, aren't I?"

I moved my hand to his cheek, "Thank you for telling me."

"It's not important."

"No, it is. We're each a vessel filled with stories. Your stories define you." I smiled at him, "And I want to hear all your stories."

His muscles relaxing, Ryon pulled me into a kiss underneath a dying oak tree. For a moment, I forgot why we came to this little rural village in the first place, but after our lips pulled away, Ryon turned back towards the road.

The village differed from the city in more than just size. Dust gathered in the air, few bushes or trees waved with green, and few people meandered throughout the streets. It reminded me of some villages I passed through in the caravan. But at least in the south, by the border, people smiled. Here, eyes remained downcast.

A tall wooden fence bordered the edge of the village. Towers stood on the corners, gaping over the town with their stern stares.

Ryon gripped my hand as he led me towards that wall, "We're here."

"Where?" I asked.

He didn't look at me. "Go to the wall and look. You'll see."

I glanced once at Ryon, then released his fingers and approached the wall. As I neared, screams bellowed from over it. My nerves galloped up my throat, and I lowered myself to a hole in the wall.

I'll never forget that moment. My heart broke into a million pieces that day. Beyond the wall, I witnessed what may have been a prison. Rows and rows of dilapidated homes filled my vision. Individuals with tattered clothing, emancipated bodies, and worn eyes worked and marched. Bodies lay in the streets, rotting. Children ran past naked.

On each of their wrists, they bore a black mark, reminiscent of the hourglass-shaped structure sitting above the Temple in the Capitol.

He stumbled back. Ryon caught me in his arms, "I got you."

"What am I looking at?"

"What do you think?" He prodded. "You wanted to make your own judgment."

"It looks like a prison!"

He touched my shoulder, nodding as he answered, "They call this the Pit. The Guard brings so-called criminals here. But that definition is flimsy; this is the home to both the murderers and the homeless, to the rapist and the magic users, and to the thieves and storytellers. They brand them and drag them here, leaving the city pristine."

"So they can say Rosada is a utopia..." I swallowed. A child ran past, playing with a handful of mud. A little further away, a man lay on the ground, hardly breathing, flies fluttering around his face. My lunch gathered in my throat. "No one deserves this..."

"I warned you."

"I know... it's just... I—" I turned away and vomited.

Evening dwindled as we made our way back to the farmhouse. We strolled in silence, clinging to each other, fear swarming. I didn't want to go home. Sweat drenched my body, my throat burned, and my eyes kept watering. How could I sleep with what lay just out of sight?

Especially alone?

"You can stay in the barn tonight if you want. That way, you don't have to go home..." Ryon mumbled. "I already have a cot set up. I spent a lot of nights in there... gets me away from my family."

"So, you do live in a barn then?" I managed a half-smile.

"Guess so." He grinned back.

The smile brought a slight pep to my step. Yet, once I returned to the barn, all I wanted was to curl up in the makeshift cot with a woolen blanket.

"I know it's been a lot..." Ryon said as I collapsed on the cot, "I understand if you want to be alone right now."

"No..." I sat up, "Stay."

"Are you sure?"

"Yes. Please."

Every time I closed my eyes, I saw the Pit. If Ryon lay next to me, maybe the nightmares wouldn't be as bad.

Perhaps I'd even feel safe.

He lowered himself onto the straw. After settling in, he removed a needle and vial from a bag beside the cot. He lifted his shirt and pressed the needle into his abdomen. I gasped as he injected the needle into his skin. He didn't even flinch, tossing the needle aside like common trash into a nearby bucket before rolling over onto his side to face me.

I took in his face, counting the freckles on his nose and observing the way his beard stuck out in uneven patches. With a single hand, I ran my fingers along his beard, then let them fall down the side of his body, and along his stomach, before leaning in for a kiss.

We lay together, entwined in each other's arms. The late summer humidity drenched us in sweat, but I didn't pull back from him, kissing him every few minutes to make sure he was there.

With each kiss, desperation wallowed in my chest. We would keep each other safe.

And Ryon responded with the same yearning.

Harder.

More passionate.

Desperate.

We tossed our worries into the affection, devouring each other while wrapped in this blanket of fear. My body craved him. My heart cried for him.

I needed him.

My hands found the buttons of his tunic. The shirt fell away, and he stared at me, stiff and wide-eyed.

"Nan..." he murmured. "I told you. I'm clueless about all this most of the time."

"That's okay. I had some people teach me..." I removed my dress, sitting before him in my bodice and stockings. I brought his fingers to the lace front, guiding him through unknotting it, allowing my chest to breathe.

He gulped, staring at me. "You had someone teach you?"

"Is that okay?"

He nodded, pivoting his gaze away.

I redirected him back at me, and I guided his hand to my skin. He trembled as his fingers circled the curves of my breasts.

"I don't know what I'm doing..." He laughed again. "Are you sure you want this?"

"Yes. I want you. I need you, Ryon Barnes. Do you want this?"

He nodded, "I do."

I leaned in to kiss him again. "Then trust me."

EIGHT

I slept wrapped in Ryon's arms, breathing in his sweat and musk as dawn trickled into the barn. We took our time getting dressed, stealing kisses every few moments, and leaning into each other as we walked across the field. Our night smoked out my worries, sending them deep into the pit of my stomach.

It was only as we ventured from the village I glimpsed the looming fence again, and my heart sank.

I gripped Ryon's wrist tight as he maneuvered his brown mare down the road. Every few minutes, I would stop him, kissing him hard to make sure he was real and that I was safe.

The horse whinnied in frustration after the third stop.

I wanted to spend all day with Ryon. If I didn't have work, we might have pulled off into the forest to make love again and never left each other's side. Sure, Ryon wasn't a skilled lover like Gisela or Yeshua, but he had loved me with all his heart the previous night. To me, that's all that mattered. And I wanted to keep that tender touch close to my heart.

As we pulled up to the Capitol building, we made a show of kissing on the steps; it was a promise to ignite change.

How?

I didn't know.

Just like I didn't realize Marietta stood right there, watching us.

As I turned away from Ryon, waving at him one last time before he rode off, I ran straight into her. My face warmed. "Oh! Marietta!"

"I had a suspicion you were with Mr. Barnes." Marietta smirked.

"Please don't tell Elodie..." I fidgeted with my dress, brushing a few pieces of straw from my skirt.

"Oh, she already has a hunch. She is not happy."

"I'm—"

"But I think it is none of her business. You're a grown, smart young woman. But..." Marietta placed an arm over my shoulder and walked me up the stairs, "you do need a fresh set of clothes. You do not want people spreading rumors. Lucky for you, I have a few extra outfits in my bag that I was taking to the tailor."

Grateful, I followed Marietta to her office and retrieved the dress. It was a tad too big for me, but it was far better than wreaking of hay and manure. Captain Oberland didn't even blink as he walked into his office, focused on rolling tobacco and chewing on the edge of his old cigar. I held my breath as I sat down at my desk. The previous day flooded back; did they discover how I altered the report? They would reprimand me!

Captain Oberland remained drawn into his work. "Ah, good morning, Doris. Are you feeling better?"

"Oh, um, quite," I replied as I pulled out my parchment and my pen, listening as the code buzzed through the telegraph machine.

...- —.- .

"VQE," I muttered to myself. This was a common abbreviation I'd seen before in several reports. It could mean anything, but I also knew what Captain Oberland's command did. They helped keep the streets of the Capitol clean of criminals...and vagrants.

VQE.

V...as in vagrant? E...as in eradicated?

Was I looking too much into it?

Captain Oberland cut off my train of thought. "Good, good, much has happened! We must get to work at once." He launched into one of his infamous rambles, "A few women were recently evicted from their homes. Did you hear about that? Well, the Guard has... They relocate... They assisted in their relocation, and these women are no longer homeless. They will be quite happy now. Oh, and also, two men were found robbing a bakery, but after an alter...but to our relief, no one was hurt, and the men returned the goods. They have since left the Capitol. All is busy, but all is well."

I brought the ink to the page and eyed Captain Oberland. Lies. They were all lies.

VQE.

Did I know the truth?

I knew more than most.

VQE... Vagrants... eradicated... It could be coincident. The codes might have meant anything.

But the Guard lied. They always lied.

Even my false histories would be more truthful.

So instead, I wrote:

Entry 850-254-01

The Guard has evicted two women from their home and relocated them to the Pit outside of the Capitol to cleanse the streets of who they consider scum. The women did no wrong.

Entry 850-254-02

Two men robbed a bakery to feed their families. An altercation ensued, and the Guard murdered both men.

I punctuated my statement, then filed the report away with the other documents. Victors, they say, write history.

Too bad the victors can't write.

"WHERE HAVE YOU BEEN?" Elodie shrieked at me as I arrived home that evening.

As much as I longed to spend all night with Ryon again, it was a necessary evil. I needed fresh clothes, and I was sure Elodie would send the Guard after Ryon if he kept me away much longer.

I swore Elodie was going to explode as I walked in the front door. Her eyes flared, her lips quivered, and her voice sliced through the air. She spent the next hour shouting over my "irresponsibility."

"You just met the man!" She screamed. "What if he killed you? Or abandoned you in the forest? Or raped you? Come now, Doris!"

I did not reply.

"I'm absolutely appalled by your behavior! Papa never would have let you stay out so late. Absolutely horrid...pah!" Elodie finished her speech.

I eyed her, holding back my tears and anger with a mere sentence. "Are you finished?"

Elodie glared.

I rose, refusing to break eye contact. "You are not in charge of me, Elodie. I am an adult."

"You live in my house!"

"Then I'll move!"

"No, you will not!"

"You're not my mother!"

"No, I'm your older sister. I want to protect you!"

"You're suffocating me!" I shouted. "I'll find a new place to live if you won't let me enjoy MY LIFE!"

She scoffed, "You haven't any money."

"I've been saving!"

"That will last you a week with a freeloader like Mr. Barnes."

"You don't know Ryon! Stop acting like you do!"

"I've seen him for years now loitering around the Capitol like some common vagrant! He wants to overthrow the government! The people he hangs out with end up disappearing... I don't want you to disappear too!"

"Because the government is corrupt!"

"That is Mr. Barnes talking. Not you! Perhaps I should take you to more services at the Temple..." Elodie trailed off as she spoke.

"No!" I clenched my fists. "You keep saying Ryon is a traitor, but have you ever thought that I agree with him? I've seen what upsets him...it upsets me too!"

"Doris—Nanette... use your head!"

"No! Maybe YOU should think for yourself and LOOK AROUND!"

"Please, I only want what is best for you..." Elodie stepped forward.

"Then leave me alone! I don't want your opinions! I just want to live my life!"

We glowered at each other for a long moment.

"Fine," Elodie broke the standoff. "I will leave you alone. Don't come to me when you get arrested."

"Fine!"

"Fine."

I huffed, then stormed upstairs and collapsed on my bed. Only the shaking windowpanes broke the thin silence in my room.

Elodie and I erected a wall between us... and it would take more than a simple apology to demolish it.

Tap. Tap. Tap.

I jolted awake to tapping on my window. Ryon waited beneath my window, tossing pebbles against the glass. Excitement flooded through my body, and I held up my hand to tell him to wait. I slipped on my slippers and tiptoed downstairs, creaking open the back door to wave him inside the house.

He greeted me with a passionate kiss.

"I couldn't sleep. I missed you." Ryon mumbled into my hair.

"I'm glad you're here."

We kissed again, then snuck into the kitchen, being careful not to wake Elodie. Rather than heading upstairs, I unlocked the door to the basement and led him downstairs. I hadn't gone down there much, really, except to retrieve bottles of liquor. But, while I went down there infrequently, Elodie never ventured down the steps.

It would make a perfect hideaway.

I lit a single lantern on the wall. The flame illuminated the rickety wood, highlighting the different colored bottles and old white draped furniture. I pulled a few of the sheets off the furniture to reveal an old bar, a shelf, and a couple of chairs. With the cloth and furniture, we erected a fort, hiding us away from any unsuspecting eyes.

As we lay on the ground, I recanted my altercation with Elodie to him.

"I am so sorry. This is all my fault..." Ryon said. "I would hate to get between you and your sister."

"It's not your fault. Elodie has been driving me crazy lately. Really. I wouldn't have it any other way..." I nuzzled my nose into his shoulder.

"Yeah, but she's right, Nan. I'm not the best person to hang around. It's amazing the government hasn't locked me in the Pit yet with how much I babble!"

"It doesn't matter to me. I want to help with this fight." I stroked his cheek, "It's my choice to make."

He kissed me again, and we fell back onto the sheets. We inhaled each other and dove into love, fueled by the rush of being caught and the want to ignite change. Each time we moaned too loud or our giggles grew too excited, we quieted each other with a gentle shush. Ryon touched me with love and respect, letting me teach him how to get me to peak before I satisfied his own needs.

I rolled off him and exhaled, sighing into him as we snuggled on the floor well into the early morning. Ryon said little as he lay beside me, twisting his fingers through my hair with my head against his chest. When he finally rolled over to face me, he spoke with a sense of curiosity and amazement. "You know what this was?"

"Hm? What what was?"

"This basement?"

I shook my head.

"It was a tavern. See the bar, and the shelving there, and the way the ceiling arches? Above must have been the sleeping house, but down here was where the magic happened..." He sat up slightly as he motioned to the fixtures. "Why wouldn't you keep this place up and running? It's a prime location! People would flock here. You'd be rich!"

"Marietta isn't the social type, and Elodie is...well, Elodie," I giggled. "And it's not my home."

"What a missed opportunity. I would love a place like this." There it was, that spark in his eyes of the farm boy who wanted to exchange his field for city lights.

"We'll find our own place like this someday," I replied.

"Nanette..." He stroked my hair back. "You know I have got no money or anything. I'm...I can't give you glamor or glitz."

"That doesn't matter. We can build our own fortress. Together. That's all I ever want."

NINE

----.

Elodie stopped talking to me.

Or perhaps I stopped talking to her.

Either way, we didn't say a word to each other as the days turned to weeks. She wrapped herself in preparing for the baby or reading her law journals while I wrapped myself in Ryon and the Capitol's lies. When we passed each other in the hallway or ran into each other in the kitchen, we behaved like the wind through the trees. Present, but invisible.

Marietta and I remained friends. On the days when Ryon couldn't take me into the city, we rode together, talking like nothing had changed. With the elixirs from the apothecary, her features became more defined, coupled with a smile that extended from cheek to cheek. She no longer resembled the sad individual staring out the window that I first met. Now, she laughed with such vigor, beaming as she stared at her own reflection in her handheld mirror before applying her pink lipstick.

At work, I continued to add slithers of truth in Captain Oberland's reports. It wasn't hard to figure out the lies. He circled around statements, backtracking on them until reaching a conclusion that sounded too simplistic or flat to be true. Often, I found secrets in the telegraphs as well, codes indicating vagrancy and attacks.

Some nights, I even dreamt of the tap-code coming through the golden plated telegraph machines.

.—. .. -

"Pit."

. .-. .- -..

"Erad," as in eradicated.

And more.

But even as I started inserting the truth into his narrative, I didn't feel quite right. I was using my imagination to fill in the blanks. Coupled with the snips of tap-code, I described the Pit, or the way women cried as the guard dragged them away, and how children played with bones rather than toys. But what if I was wrong? What if I was the liar?

I often whispered my concerns to Ryon at night. He told me, each time, that I could stop.

But I couldn't.

I wouldn't.

Not after what I saw.

I spent every evening with Ryon. Some days, we explored the city, where Ryon would detail the histories of different buildings, or we would venture to the Black Market to listen to stories. Other times, we would go back to the farmhouse, where his family welcomed me with a hearty meal before we vanished into the barn. On others, he snuck into Elodie's home, where we hid in the basement. Or we rode his buggy off into the woods to make love until the moon hung high.

I often worried our flame would diminish, but instead of leaving scorch marks, it flickered like an eternal light.

Everything continued in my favor. Ryon's father allowed him to continue his work for the time being, and I saved money to move out of Elodie's home. By the birth of the New Year, I would be free of Elodie's glare.

I'd be free to be myself.

Things were going well, I had to say. Really. My civil act of rebellion had gone unnoticed; hints of the truth were working their way into the heart of the Capitol.

Ryon was by my side through it all.

I should have known something would give.

And that's when Jaida Heartz entered the narrative.

I remember it well. The brisk autumn air bit at my face as I climbed out of Ryon's buggy, kissing him firmly on the lips. He draped his coat over my shoulders before vanishing down the road to complete his daily route. I always watched him leave on days when he took me to work, smiling to myself over the way the breeze caught his curls before turning towards the Capitol.

Nothing seemed different that day. Like all other days, when I arrived in Captain Oberland's office, I started my housekeeping, filing away papers, recording the telegraphs, and humming to myself. The captain hadn't arrived yet, but I didn't mind. During these hours, I rewrote old memos, correcting parts where Captain Oberland discussed the utopian elements of the city and the human nature of relocation. A rush came with each treasonous act. If the Guard caught me, I might end up in the Pit myself.

But many crimes are worse than forgery.

Besides, no one could identify the authors of these old memos. Yes, I was Captain Oberland's scribe, but there were others before me and others now who sometimes stepped in my place. We each followed a standard handwritten scrawl, each letter identical to the next; it would take a lot to indict me by my handwriting alone.

I made sure not to alter every memo and record. There were simpler ones that didn't require my invasion: guards watching over the farmer's market, a woman arrested for murder, and other heart-wrenching events that resulted in death. These were the documents Captain Oberland spoke about in confidence, and I had telegraphs to confirm those tales.

That day though, as I completed a few statements, a knock pulled me from my work.

"Enter!" I called from my desk.

A dark round woman strode into the room while pulling her dark, frizzy hair pulled back into an even bun. She raised one eyebrow at me. "Captain... Oberland?"

I rose to greet the woman. "Oh, no. I'm his scribe, Nanette Ivans. Captain Oberland isn't in right now. Is there anything I can help you with?"

"My name is Jaida Heartz. I am Senator Heartz's sister and assistant."

I was sure Ryon had mentioned Senator Heartz to me at one point. He told me about all the different senators' names and stances, but I often couldn't keep up with him. I was still learning all the ins and outs of Rosada; I did only immigrate a few months earlier.

For posterity's sake, I merely nodded to Ms. Heartz.

Jaida went straight to the point. "My brother would like reports on the Utopia Project. I heard Captain Oberland oversaw this endeavor."

"The Utopia Project..." I whispered. My mind flared, my heart raced. I'd never heard of it before, nor had I seen anything in telegraphs. But I had a guess. "You mean... why we don't have any criminals or vagrants in the city?"

"Yes." Jaida stared hard at me.

"Why does the senator need this information, may I ask?"

"It isn't public knowledge yet, but the Senate is examining this project to implement it across the nation. My brother wants to understand the matter before casting his vote. Do you think you can help?"

My mind pounded. So, the rest of the senators didn't know about the Pit? Did that mean there was hope for it to end? Or was her brother the type who would support it?

I considered my options. Should I hand over my memos? Should I wait for Captain Oberland to arrive?

I finally replied. "Yes. If you would like, I can reserve a spot for you next week on the captain's calendar?"

Jaida sighed, "That'll be too late. I'll ask someone else. Thank you, nonetheless."

"Wait!" I jumped. Could this be my only chance to set things right?

She glanced at me.

"I have not been told all the information, but I have some memos from the past three months that might help."

"Oh?"

I removed a pile of documents from the drawer. "These are all Captain Oberland's reports over the last couple months regarding his progress. The Historical Records Departments file them every quarter. I can put in an inquiry for you for more details...as well as for the Utopia Project."

Jaida took the memos from me and nodded. "I'll start with these. If you could submit that request, it would be quite helpful. Thank you, Miss Ivans."

I nodded, feeling quite small beneath her steady gaze.

And with that, Jaida Heartz left, carrying my pile of treasonous truths.

The rest of the day passed in a blur. I submitted a request for the Utopia Project files, but other than that, I operated in a daze. It all happened so fast! What was I thinking? For all I knew, Senator Heartz might be in favor of this Utopia, a puppet placed by the Order, preaching to ban stories and magic.

As soon as I finished, I raced out of the Capitol. Ryon waited for me on the steps. Rather than greeting him with my usual kiss, I tugged him into an alleyway.

Once I was sure no one followed, I bombarded him with questions. "Ryon, please tell me everything you know about Senator Heartz! Does he support storytellers? What is his stance on magic? Is he on our side?"

"Nanette, Nanette, relax!" Ryon kneaded my shoulders. "I've never seen you this flustered."

"You don't understand..." I explained in haste everything that happened. "I wasn't certain what to do, but it might get the word out. So, I thought, why not? But now I'm worried it might implicate me."

Ryon chuckled, "Nan, I've talked about Senator Heartz plenty."

"You talk about a lot of senators!" I protested.

"Yeah, well, Senator Heartz is one of the best. He is not an Order Puppet. The senator and his sister are probably some of the best people in that building... other than you, of course." He winked.

I relaxed, "Oh... thank goodness."

He nudged my chin. "Just be a bit more careful. You're risking your boss finding out... or worse. I don't want you to get hurt."

"It's part of my rebellion."

He grinned so his gold tooth flashed in the light. "Yeah, you're on fire like a sunset, Nanette. But, please, don't burn yourself to the ground."

"I'll be careful. I promise."

We kissed, then arm-in-arm, strode down the road away from the Capitol. The stories beckoned us from the Black Market. As we walked, Ryon inspected every little detail of my meeting with Jaida. He asked about her voice, to the way she moved. He spoke with such excitement; it was like listening to a child talk about their favorite animal or food. But a twinge of fear continued on his tongue. *What if I got in trouble? What would he do if I were in danger?* I couldn't picture Ryon yielding a pistol or blade.

Perhaps we'd run away. Would that be the worst thing?

The usual mist whistling through the city grew thicker as we approached the Black Market's usual corner. It pooled from our feet, clamored into the air, creating a black film that blinded us with ash. I squinted through it as the smoke wrapped its steel fingers around me.

There, like demon shadows, stood a squadron of Guards. They stared me down, eyes narrow.

I recognized their insignia.

They belonged to Captain Oberland.

Ryon approached them, trying to steal a glance down the alleyway. "What's going on? We were trying to cut through..."

"None of your concern, kid," the dark-eyed guard in charge snarled. "Move along."

Ryon tiptoed to see over their heads. "Usually, it's so empty down there..."

"I said move along, kid!"

"Ryon, come on. Let's go. It's not worth it." I tugged on his sleeve.

"Yeah, well, I think it's our right to know what's going on, don't you think?" His eyes flared. It was that determined look, the curious look.

The one that Elodie said bore danger.

The one that Ryon said got him in trouble.

But I didn't fear it.

Ryon continued talking to the Guard. "C'mon. Just wanna make sure there's nothing to worry about or anything."

The Guard shoved him back. Ryon hit the ground. Hard.

"I told ya to get a move on, kid." The Guard jammed his steel-toed boot into Ryon's face.

I screamed.

He kicked again.

I pulled Ryon away from the Guard after the third kick. His entire face dripped with blood from his nose and mouth.

"We're leaving," I said. "Come on, Ryon."

"Tell your fucker that he better stay in line. I doubt he wants to end up like the rest of them." The Guard bellowed.

I didn't stick around to question the Guard. If Ryon was in his right mind, he would have... but I didn't want to test fate. Instead, I helped him off the ground, glanced back once at the Guard, then led Ryon out of the alleyway.

"Fuckers..." He grunted as we collapsed on the side of the road.

I pulled a kerchief from my skirt pocket and dabbed his face. "That was ridiculous..."

"I know! How could they—"

"No! You! What were you thinking? They might have killed you!"

"I was thinking they destroyed the market! All our storytellers... our friends!" Ryon gritted his teeth.

"Maybe they escaped..."

"But we don't know that." Ryon wiped the blood away from his face. "I get I was being dumb, but I needed to find out. Now it's just gonna be another false history for the books. We'll never know..."

"We can't assume anything—"

"Cause it makes an ass out of you and me?" Ryon joked.

I stroked back his hair and smiled. "Yes. But also... those are Captain Oberland's men. I can find out tomorrow what the false story is. Because even if they got rid of the market, stories never truly vanish."

TEN

`.---- -----`

Ryon stayed the night at Elodie's place with me, deep in the basement in our usual fort. I cleaned his face well, despite his nose not sitting quite right, then I helped him with his daily injection. He winced as I pricked his skin too deep with the needle but then relaxed, settling on the floor. The moment he lay down, he passed out, horrid snores echoing around the cellar. He would need something from the apothecary to heal for good.

He was still asleep when I woke the next morning. To my relief, Elodie had left for the day to attend a service at the Temple, so Marietta and I took a cabby to work. I spent the ride fretting over Ryon. His breathing kept me awake most of the night.

But by the time I reached the Capitol Building, my attention focused on one thing: Captain Oberland's report.

I bid Marietta farewell, then departed to my office. Captain Oberland wasn't there yet.

But Jaida waited for me.

"Oh, hello, Ms. Heartz..." My stomach churned. "How can I help you today?"

"I read through these memos." She paced around the room as she spoke, not meeting my gaze.

"Oh."

"Is this what the captain actually said?"

"Um..." My hands grew clammy as I fiddled with the fringe of my dress.

Jaida held up her hand. "You're not in trouble if it isn't. But you clearly have more information to share. Would it be possible for us to discuss these memos in more detail?"

"Oh, um, well," I stuttered, "I should probably be here when Captain Oberland arrives."

"Yes, yes, of course! I shouldn't get ahead of myself. We can discuss this over our midday meal if that is easier?"

"Oh, um, yes. That would be lovely."

"Excellent. I'll meet you on the steps at high noon."

Jaida turned, punctuating her statement, then strutted from the room with such confidence she might have belonged to the Guard. There was reject her.

I watched her leave. She was a striking woman who commanded a room with her beauty, intelligence, and poise. Yet even her elegance did little to quell my nerves, and I hurried into my daily tasks, trying my best to keep down the bile rising in my throat.

Captain Oberland arrived an hour later. Exhaustion dripped on his face, but he still produced that usual bushy-lipped smile. "Ah, Doris. Good morning!"

"Hello, Captain Oberland." I bowed my head.

He collapsed in his chair and propped his feet up on his desk. It didn't take long for him to ramble about the previous day. Per usual, most statements were dry and uninteresting, detailing how his men completed their rounds and monitored suspicious activity. I wrote in haste, not bothering to backtrack any of the statements, eager for anything about the Black Market.

Impatience fluttered in me as his usual ramblings dragged.

Until finally, he reached the end of the day.

"Yesterday evening, we located a potential Black Market in the heart of the Capitol. We have not found the perpetrators yet, though. In the meantime, we stationed guards in triplicate around the city, and we hope to end this villainous Black Market without bloodshed." His sentences were firm, woven together like a knitted blanket. He didn't flinch.

My body relaxed as I punctuated the statement. They had hurt no one *yet*.

Well, except for Ryon.

I dropped the quill and leaned back in my seat. "Is that everything for today, Captain Oberland?"

"Yes, I believe so. Thank you, Doris. You're always fantastic."

Guilt cooled my bones. For a moment, I almost felt sorry for using Captain Oberland's name in treason. But... he was lying for the Order. Even the nicest guard was still a guard; even *he* sanctioned murder.

"I hope I'll continue to make you proud," I whisper, stuffing down the bile in my throat.

"Ah, yes." His face hardened for a second, but like when he wove his fallacies, his persona changed in an instant. "Well, I shall see you tomorrow! I have quite a few meetings today. Please, if time permits, allow yourself to leave early, Doris. It's a wonderful Autumn day."

"Thank you, Captain Oberland. I shall try."

He left the room so I could complete the memo. I altered nothing. This time, at least, he spoke nothing but the truth.

A little before noon, I exited the Capitol Building to meet Jaida. She wasn't anywhere to be seen. To my surprise, Ryon waited on the steps, holding a basket of food.

"Ryon!" I threw my arms around him and kissed his cheeks.

He winced. "Ow! Dammit, Nan, my face hurts still."

"Sorry..." I flushed and pecked his cheek, lighter this time. "Did you leave the house, okay?"

"No one was home, so yeah. I did. Couldn't get the horse to wake up, though. He liked sleeping in the field near the house."

I giggled, snagging an apple out of the basket to take a bite. Ryon watched me, exhaustion creeping over his face as he chewed on his bottom lip. A bruise settled on his nose, and he winced every time he wrinkled it while his nostrils whistled an irregular tune.

It didn't stop him from asking questions. "Did you find anything out?"

I swallowed a mouthful of apple and nodded. "Yes. It was just a watch last night. They were trying to smoke people out but found nothing. Captain Oberland didn't flinch...so I could tell it was the truth. The storytellers are safe today."

Ryon sighed with relief.

I leaned into him. "See? You did not need to get in that Guard's face."

"Eh, he might've deserved it." He shrugged, "We need to get the word out tonight, though."

I nodded and took another bite of my apple.

We huddled on the steps in silence, eating pieces of fruit until Jaida emerged from the Capitol Building. "Ah! Miss Ivans!"

I clamored to my feet and brushed off my dress. "Oh! Ms. Heartz!"

"Please, call me Jaida." She smiled. "Who's your friend here?"

Ryon rose beside me, fidgeting with the cuffs of his shirt as he spoke. "Ms. Heartz! Hi! I've heard a lot about you and your brother. I'm a huge supporter! I've read about everything you are proposing. And I absolutely love the idea of building a railway track through the province to make transportation more accessible and—oh, right, where are my manners?" His face reddened. "My name is Ryon Barnes, by the way. Like a barn. The big red buildings by the farms. But I'm a human. Um...sorry. I just can't believe I'm meeting you!"

Jaida didn't seem phased by Ryon's fumbling statement. "It is a pleasure to meet you, Mr. Barnes! It is quite rare to find someone so supportive of my brother and me in the Capitol."

Ryon didn't stop grinning.

I redirected the conversation before Ryon threatened to derail it further. As much as I loved Ryon, I knew if he launched into a tangent, breaking it would be harder than cutting wood with a spoon. "You wanted to speak with me?"

"Ah yes, the memos. Come, let us talk away from here." Jaida motioned me away from the steps.

Ryon shuffled in his spot.

"You may come along too, Mr. Barnes. If Miss Ivans can trust you, then I suppose I can as well, so I might as well pick your brain.

Another smile lit up Ryon's face.

We followed Jaida to a café in the plaza. This was Ryon's dream: to talk to someone with such high governmental standing had to make him giddy. In another life, he may have even been a politician, but he didn't have the education or mindset to join politics. A shame, really. He would have made a great leader.

Jaida glanced over her shoulder a few times as she pulled the memos out of her bag. New scribbles of red ink detailed their margins.

Vertigo settled in with a bout of queasiness, and I stumbled forward. Ryon guided me into a chair before crouching down and placing his own hand on my knee to calm me.

"I asked you this already, but I just want to confirm... this isn't what Captain Oberland said, is it?" Jaida asked.

I shook my head.

"That's what I thought. No guard as seasoned as Captain Oberland would implicate himself like this. So, just to confirm, you wrote these?"

I hesitated, then nodded.

"You realize perjury is illegal, don't you? I do not want to give my brother information when I am not one-hundred percent certain that it is true. Can you prove any of this?"

I stared. If I dared speak, I might have puked in Jaida's face.

Ryon came to my rescue. "I can show you the Pit."

"The Pit?"

"Yeah, the Pit. Haven't you heard about it? I think it has to do with that Utopia Project you requested information on—" He flushed again, "Sorry... I probably shouldn't know about that."

Jaida's eyes narrowed.

"I know. It sounds crazy. But listen, the Pit will prove everything Nanette has written is true. I can show you! Please... Nan is just trying to do right, is all..." Ryon glanced at me. I couldn't meet his gaze. My mind raced. Would Jaida turn me over to the Guard? Was I about to be thrown into the Pit myself?

Jaida put the memos back into her pocket, "Show me."

"Of course," Ryon said as he squeezed my knee. His knuckles turned white. While I was busy suffocating on my fear, Ryon must have battled his own nerves. He never spoke with any politician, only about them, and now the one he admired wanted his help. I could only imagine the way his head spun.

Jaida rose, "Excellent. Thank you, Mr. Barnes. I have a few things to wrap up, so I'll meet you back here in an hour if that is agreeable?"

"Yes, of course. I'll get my buggy."

"Wonderful," Jaida turned, then stopped and stared at me straight, "And Miss Ivans?"

"Yes?" I squeaked.

"Be careful. If these memos got into the wrong hands, your life could be on the line."

Ryon and I had the rest of the lunch hour to ourselves. In a fit of excitement, we found ourselves in a quiet corner where we could kiss, celebrating our minor moment of rebellion with each other and no one else.

I rested my head against Ryon's side as we clung to each other. If work wasn't beckoning me, we might have gone back home to succumb to our desperate emotions. For now, we held each other, holding on to the constant reminder that one wrong move could end all of this.

"Is this going to be worth it?" I asked Ryon as he walked me back to the Capitol Building.

"Yes." He said and kissed me again. "I'll see you later, okay?"

I nodded as I turned, only to pause and glance back at him, "I love you."

The words tumbled out of my mouth so quick, I didn't believe I had said them at first. But it was the truth.

I really loved him.

His face turned red. "Yeah?"

"Yes."

"Well, I love you too."

I blew him a kiss before heading into the building, brushing past Jaida as I headed down the hall. We nodded once, and with a smile on my face, I strolled back for Captain Oberland's office.

The door hung open as I approached. Did Captain Oberland forget something? Did they move one of his meetings into his office? I peeked inside the door.

But Captain Oberland wasn't waiting for me.

Instead, a man with a pointed face and dark eyes sat on the corner of my desk.

I recognized him.

He broke Ryon's nose.

I hoped he didn't recognize me. It had been dark out. Surely, I was just an unfamiliar face then.

"Hello, Miss Ivans," the man said.

"Sir..." I lowered my head.

"That is Captain Cordova to you."

"Cordova..." I recognized that name. My mind raced, searching for my memories. As I examined his face, I realized whom those eyes resembled. "Are you related to Elder Vic Tor, sir?"

"Smart lass. He's my brother." The captain leaned back.

I gulped, trying my best to keep myself together. "What can I do for you... Captain Cordova?"

"I have come to inform you that Captain Oberland retired today. As of today, I am taking over his charge."

I blinked and furrowed my brow. "I didn't know Captain Oberland was planning to retire..."

"It was quite a sudden retirement, I say. Perhaps you can shed some light on why he would decide to leave..." Captain Cordova paced around me, his eyes unflinching, like a hawk. "We asked him to clarify his request for classified documents. He didn't provide many details. I assume you wrote that request for him?"

"Which one?" I already expected the answer.

"There was a request filed to retrieve a report about the so-called Utopia Project."

"Utopia Project? I don't recall..." I feigned confusion.

"Yes, the Utopia Project. Pray tell, why would he want those confidential documents?"

"Oh, no, I'm sorry, I'm not sure." I kept my gaze on Captain Cordova. "He must have just asked me to request them, and I filed it away in haste. He was quite the busy man."

"Is that so?"

"Yes."

"Very well." Captain Cordova paced the room. "I hope you will honor my requests just as you honored Captain Oberland's. Because perjury is a treasonous offense. Is that understood?"

"Yes, sir."

The sky bled as I left work. I couldn't get the day's events out of my head. What happened to Captain Oberland? Did he take the fall for me? Or did he really believe he requested the files? Would I ever see him again?

I didn't know.

It ached my heart, knowing how much I used the old man to my advantage. He was always kind to me. A liar, perhaps, but kind at least. He didn't overwork me and never belittled me. I was his equal.

Captain Cordova, I already could tell, wasn't like that. Even after working for him for half the day, I felt violated. He watched every move I made with his eyes constantly open like an owl. I worried that if I dared break my pen or write the wrong word, he would scream. I did not speak, I did not dare lie, and I did not flinch. As soon as I finished my work, I punctuated my statements and filed them with haste, yearning to escape his constant watch.

Ryon didn't wait for me on the steps as I expected. He and Jaida were probably still on their way back from the Pit. I considered waving down another cabby to head home, but my heart ached too much. I needed to confide in Ryon.

And I certainly didn't need to sit at home with Elodie.

Every noise in the street, every buggy, and every horse whinnying caused me to jump. I couldn't shake the feeling that someone was watching me. The lights from the watchtowers in the distance formed eyes in the cloudy skies.

Did they watch my movement with everyone else? After all, in the Capitol, are you ever truly alone?

I gulped as I glanced back at the Capitol one last time. I needed to warn the storytellers still about the Guard. The smoke out might have been enough to alert them, but like any act of rebellion, fear cannot hinder it.

My feet carried me through the city, towards the alleyway where the Black Market often wove its way into the stone. Magic cast a protective void over it, and to my surprise and relief, no guards lurked nearby. The street, like any other day, bustled with storytellers, magic, and children playing. Entering that alleyway was like magic itself. My shoulders relaxed, and my bout of paranoia vanished.

Stories whisked me away and provided comfort. For a bit, I forgot why I came to the Black Market. I got lost in a tale about a mermaid and a pirate, then danced as someone sang about dragons. One pyromancer created images out of flames. It took me back to my father's deathbed where, in his last few days of life, he spoke of dragons and adventure. They served as an opportunity to escape the ultimate curse of death.

And now, they gave me a chance to abandon my troubles.

Lucidity washed over me, and I found the words in my throat. While I tipped each storyteller, I whispered a warning about the Guard and their Utopia Project. The storytellers would nod, then vanish into the crowd, while I became enamored by another tale. They didn't seem too afraid.

Did they always live with this constant fear?

Or, like me, did stories offer them a chance to escape?

Listening to all these stories caused time to disappear in the Black Market, though. I loved each tale, clinging to each one with fascination.

But as I paid more attention to the stories, I lost my attention to detail.

If I had been more alert, I might have noticed the signs. I ventured into my fantasies, pretending that the Black Market was untouchable. Even now, despite the Guards the other day, we were unstoppable. The Storytellers knew now about the danger.

Would the Guards even come?

But in the back of my mind, I understood that wasn't the case.

Had I kept those fears front and center, I might have been able to save them.

If I had spoken my warning in haste, they might have fled.

Instead, I placed a coin in an old woman's hand as she finished her story of a girl and a goat. I leaned forward to offer my quiet warning.

Despite everything I learned, it didn't prepare me for what happened next.

It didn't prepare anyone.

A low grumble rocked the alleyway. The music screeched to a halt. Everything stopped.

I turned.

There were no guards.

No gunshots.

And then, without a moment's notice, the walls surrounding the Black Market exploded.

All I saw was orange.

ELEVEN

.---- .----

Everything hurt.

I couldn't open my eyes. When I breathed, I choked.

Someone held my hand. They said my name.

Eventually, I spoke. "Ryon?"

"I'm here. I'm here." He pushed back my hair. "You're alright."

"What happened?" I squinted at him.

"There was an explosion. You were in the Black Market when it all happened..." Ryon stroked my cheek again. "I saw it all. Happened right when I got back with Jaida. You got so lucky, Nan."

"I was trying to warn them... but they brushed it off..." I coughed.

"They hear these warnings a lot. After a while, they ignore them."

"But did anyone survive?"

"I got some kids out. Ran right in as soon as I could. Others were helping, too. Some big fellow was carrying you on his back when I finally found you. Didn't catch

his name, but...he saved your life. Nanette... I thought..."
He closed his eyes and squeezed my hand, his voice
breaking, "I thought I lost you."

I reached for him, "I'm here."

"I know... but...you could have died." He shook his
head. "I can't believe Captain Oberland issued the order...you always said that he was a kind man and—"

"Captain Oberland isn't in charge anymore..." I slowly
detailed the events that took place earlier in the day. My
throat hurt by the end, but I gulped back my tears.

"That explains it then. They...this Cordova fellow...he
must have issued the order." Ryon seethed. "The Black
Market is destroyed! They killed so many people, and
you...you were so lucky, Nanette."

He gathered me in his arms, gentle as always, and
held me close. His entire body shook.

"I'm fine," I promised. My body still ached, but as far
as I could tell, it was just a few bumps and bruises. Otherwise, I survived.

Ryon's fear rocked the room. "I...I can't lose you.
Nanette...I know it hasn't been long...but you...I love
you, and I don't know what I would do if I lost you..."

I stroked his cheek, running my fingers through his
beard. "We'll get through this. We're going to be alright.
Because I love you too."

"But... it's just... I can't... I can't lose you," Ryon repeated.

"You never will." I pulled him close. "We're going to get our own place once we have the money, and then we can get married and never be apart again."

Ryon shifted backward to stare at me. "Married?"

"What?" My face warmed. "Haven't you considered it?"

"Yes...but...are you...is this a proposal?" Ryon laughed.

"It can be."

"Well, then...yes! Of course, I want to marry you! Just...this is...unexpected!" He laughed nervously. "Yes! We should get married once everything is stable. Yes! Yes! Yes!" His voice squeaked on each note. "You'll marry me?"

"That's what I said!"

"We're not moving too fast, though? We've only known each other for a couple of months—"

"Marietta and Elodie were engaged within a month. But if it makes you feel better, we can say it's a tentative proposal. Until we're ready." I took his hand and kissed it.

"Until we feel ready... yes. Yes! That's perfect. You're perfect!" He swooped me up in his arms and kissed me deeply. I shifted under the flurrying heat of the kiss, but the aches and pains stopped me from pushing further.

We kept kissing until the door swung open.

"Now that's utterly absurd!" Elodie's voice boomed. "How dare you take advantage of my sweet sister when she's injured, of all things?"

Ryon released me.

Elodie waltzed into the room, carrying a tray of food and water. She glowered. "What a ruckus you got yourself into, Doris Nanette Ivans! I told you those storytellers were no good!"

"What?" I sat up again, using Ryon's arm for support.

"It's in all the gazettes! They say the storytellers wanted to tell a tale about fire demons, so they set the alleyway ablaze! They killed people! Nanette, you could have been one of them!" Elodie shoved a piece of bread and the glass of water into my hands. "You are fortunate to end up only with a couple cuts."

I stared at her. "The storytellers didn't cause the explosion. The Guard did."

"Oh, you must have hit your head hard, dear." Elodie took my hands. "The Guard were only there to stop people from getting hurt."

"I was there! I saw! None of the storytellers were doing anything wrong! The Guard trapped us and set the alley ablaze!"

"No, they didn't! Mr. Barnes is filling your head with lies."

"I saw it!"

Elodie scoffed, "Doris—"

"My name is Nanette!"

"Fine, *Nanette*. I wish you would stop with these tales and rumors. Think of the utter legal mess if the Guard was responsible! All the cover-up and details—"

"I transcribed the cover-ups!"

"Nanette—"

"You only learned about all of this bull in your law classes, which you didn't even finish!"

Elodie tossed back her hair and laughed nervously, "You're being hysterical right now!"

"I'm not!" I wanted to scream, but tears burned my cheeks, and my throat roared in aches.

Ryon came to my rescue. "Why don't you listen to your sister, Ms. Lieu? Don't you trust your family?"

"Nanette has a pension for stories and bad decisions. *Just like you.*" Elodie glared. "Why don't you go back to wooing random women and stop infiltrating my life?"

"Your life!?!" I shot up. "YOUR LIFE? Ryon is part of MY LIFE! He has done nothing to me! We love each other, Elodie, and...and we're going to get married!" My hand gripped Ryon's arm.

"No, you're not. As your older sister, I will not allow it." Elodie stated.

"Why? You don't control me!"

"I need to look out for you...for Father's sake—"

"I looked after Father for years WITHOUT you!"

Elodie shook her head. "You're disoriented, Nanette."

"I'm fine!"

"No, you're not."

"Why can't you just be happy for me, Elodie?" My voice boomed around the room. Tears cascaded down my cheeks. "I came here to be with you—my sister! But ever since I've come, all you've tried to do is make me be YOU. The moment I acted like ME, you disowned me! Why? Why can't you be happy that I've found someone that makes me smile?"

"You don't know him!" Elodie snapped.

"I know him plenty! It's you I don't know!" I tugged at the sheets as I looked away. "I guess I never realized that you were such a...such a..."

"Such a what?" Elodie's eyes flared.

I let the words escape my mouth, hissing like a snake as they escaped: "A bitch."

A moment of silence followed.

Then a smack.

It slammed into my face, numbing my jaw and leaving my mouth agape.

Elodie stared at me with her hand raised. A beat. A pause. Then, without another word, she left the room.

I said nothing as she left, unable to move. Ryon mimicked my silence as we listened to her shoes click down the hallway. Another door slammed.

All fell quiet.

Except for my sobs.

I never went back to work. The two weeks that circumvented my recovery spun in a whirlwind, resulting in a letter on our doorstep from Captain Cordova finalizing my termination. The reasoning: excessive absences. A fair reason, and I didn't bother fighting it. I couldn't tell him how I ended up injured. The questions would be relentless: *Why were you in the alleyway? Are you a storyteller? You requested those classified documents, didn't you?*

It was for the best. Why would I want to work for such an abrasive man, anyway?

Ryon stayed by my side through it all, rarely leaving. He ignored Elodie's remarks, sleeping beside me while I healed, bringing me food, and recanting current events. When I needed comfort, he kissed me tenderly. My honest, sweet fiancé; I wished for Elodie to open her heart to him so much.

At least Marietta didn't mind Ryon. In fact, I'd say she adored having another helping hand around the house. It gave her a chance to tend to Elodie's incessant demands and arrange for the baby while Ryon prepared food, completed housework, and ran errands. Every couple days, Marietta would give Ryon an elixir she acquired from her apothecary to help with my injuries, where they'd make small talk about the day-to-day. It was what I yearned for Ryon and Elodie to have; why did she have to glare at him with such hatred? What had he ever done?

Part of me understood she blamed Ryon for my injuries. Yet, she wouldn't listen to my side of the story! Every remark out of her mouth to Ryon began with, "Well, if you actually cared about Nanette, then..." before speaking in my place.

What would Papa say? He would be so happy for my engagement but so heartbroken over my feud with Elodie. Family was everything to him. We were all part of the same story, a key part of our history. But I couldn't fix the bridge between us, no matter how hard I tried.

After receiving my termination letter, I hid in my bedroom for the day, eating the chocolate cakes Ryon picked up and avoiding the mashed potatoes Elodie tried to serve me. What was I going to do? Honestly, working as a scribe had been the perfect job for me. Sure, I didn't want to work under Captain Cordova... but what could I do now?

Was my small act of rebellion worth it?

The question lingered for a few days, both aloud to Ryon and in my head. How could I help storytellers? Was I nothing more than any other civilian out there now, trying my best to survive? Was it my job to help? I was just a single person in a city; could my little statements, my little dreams, really change the world?

I fought my self-deprecation. Of course, the fight was worth it! Sometimes glory came by quiet steps, even on burned paths.

The unburned path showed itself to me when Jaida Heartz came to visit me a couple days later.

Ryon and I sat in the lounge, drinking tea like an old married couple, when a knock rocked the room. Marietta and Elodie had gone to the market. So with only the two of us there, Ryon answered the door. "Oh! Ms. Heartz!"

"I heard what happened. May I come in?"

Before Ryon could reply, Jaida pushed into the room, looking as stunning as ever. She locked eyes with me. "Oh my dear, you look terrible! I was completely heartbroken when I found out what happened."

I rose, my days of defensiveness against Elodie sticking to my tongue. "The storytellers didn't light the street aflame! It was the Guard—"

"I am quite aware." Jaida sat across from me on the couch. "I am not a fool. Ryon showed me the Pit. I understand everything now."

Right. The Pit. I had forgotten. In fact, I hadn't even asked Ryon how it went! It seemed so small in the grand scheme of things.

Jaida continued, "My brother requested the files regarding the Utopia Project. I should have had him do it in the first place, but he is quite a busy fellow. He didn't think it was relevant. It makes more sense anyway... they cannot deny a senator's request." She took my hand. "I am so sorry, Nanette. If I had used my head, you might have avoided termination."

"It's alright. I don't want to work for Captain Cordova, anyway." That was a partial lie. I imagined all the secrets I missed out on now, far away from the Capitol's walls. Still, the idea of sitting in the same room as Captain Cordova made my stomach churn.

"It is probably for the best," Jaida replied. "I heard they fired Captain Oberland without pension for *betraying* the state."

My heart sank.

Jaida continued, "I know what you are thinking, but it is not your fault. They never got a hold of your memos. I withdrew all of them for our own research. Ryon mentioned how long you've been doing this, and we decided it was best."

Ryon smiled sheepishly at me. What a gem.

Jaida continued, "Do not hold yourself accountable. In fact, they terminated Captain Oberland for his request of the Utopian Project files...a classified program. He confessed to it all."

"He...protected me?" I gasped. "Why?"

"Because he wasn't a bad fellow. When I was a child, he was a guard in the Newbird's Arm before relocating here." Jaida stared out the window. "I spoke with him briefly after his termination. He's going back to the Newbird Region to live out the rest of his life. He wanted me to tell you to stay brave."

I covered my mouth to hold back tears again. All those times working with my head down, writing those fake memos, and keeping a heart-felt smile, I never expected that Captain Oberland cared for me.

Did he know what I was doing this whole time?

Ryon massaged my back as I swallowed my tears.

"You are quite brave, Nanette. Your fight is only just beginning. I'm sure you will continue to be prosperous." Jaida said. "If I know my brother, he'll take my recommendation to heart. That's why I need someone who can help me navigate these uncertain times. Unfortunately, while I would love your assistance, I cannot justify hiring you as an aid. But..." She glanced at Ryon. "Mr. Barnes, I might persuade the committee to hire you if you are interesting. I need more information regarding the Pit, and I am sure my brother will as well, and you seem quite knowledgeable on the predicament outside the Capitol."

Ryon's eyes widened. "Really? You would take me? I'm a farm boy. I can't write well, nor do I have a formal education. Are you sure you want to hire me?"

Jaida held up her hand. "It doesn't matter. You have the information I need, and I can trust you, and that is the key."

Ryon glanced at me for reassurance. I nodded eagerly. This was what Ryon had wanted! He'd be able to stop being a cabby and move into the city... and work in the government, changing it all from within their walls! We'd be able to afford our own home soon enough... and then I would never have to bother Elodie again!

"Um, yes!" Ryon beamed. "I'd be happy to help!"

"Excellent!" Jaida smiled at both of us. "I will see you tomorrow at the Capitol Building, Mr. Barnes." She rose, then before turning, she stared at me straight with her auburn eyes. "Do not fret, Nanette. Your story will flourish soon enough."

The moment she left, I threw my arms around Ryon and squeezed him. I hadn't seen him smile like that in weeks. It lit up his eyes, punctuating his dimples, while his single golden tooth glimmered in the dim light.

I would have kissed him, but the front door swung open again. Elodie and Marietta walked into the foyer.

Elodie gagged upon seeing Ryon embrace me.

To make a point, I kissed Ryon's cheek, then released him.

"Absolutely abhorrent," Elodie snarled, "I hope you two were behaving when Ms. Heartz was here!"

They must have run into her on their way up the walk.

"Why was Jaida here, anyway?" Marietta inquired. "She usually isn't the most sociable type. Getting her to submit expense reports is a headache as it is...but she has time to come out here?"

Now was my chance to brag about my wonderful fiancé. A grin of delight on my face with each word. "Ms. Heartz just offered Ryon a job!"

I don't think I ever saw Elodie look so disgusted.

TWELVE

.---- ..---

I struggled to occupy myself the first couple weeks of Ryon's new job. Often, I paced about the house like a ghost. Ryon took up residency in the house, almost never returning back to the farm, despite Elodie's distaste. At first, she tried changing the locks on him, but Marietta had none of it. This home had belonged to the Lieu family since they immigrated here from across the seas, Marietta said, and it had always been a home for members of the family. Whether Elodie liked it or not, Ryon would someday be a part of our family.

Without a doubt, Elodie didn't like it at all. She and I avoided each other all day, and whenever she saw Ryon, I swore she cursed under her breath. For my own health, I didn't confront her. Instead, I stayed in my room until midday when Elodie left to go shopping for the baby. While I didn't mind the silence, using the time to recollect my thoughts, I also tiptoed about my loneliness, wrapping myself in reveries about times without trouble or fear.

I dreamt of days when my father was still alive, when Elodie and I were friends hiding from our mother's disgusting casserole, and when stories were free.

But often, I thought about my future with Ryon: our wedding, our future home, and our adventures.

After finding out about our engagement, Ryon's family threw a wonderful shindig down on their farm. People from all over the village came to congratulate us and wish us good prosperity. Even his father smiled while his mother and sisters danced around the village fountain, throwing ribbons around us in excitement.

While each interaction sent my head spinning, I lavished in meeting the rest of Ryon's family. His uncle ran the brewery in the village, often delivering crates of ale to the guards as they sat perched along the Pit's wall. The beer was plenty during the party, and on the back of liquid ecstasy, I forgot my worries. For a while, I felt like I was part of a family again.

But even the alcohol did little to take away the pang in my heart for Elodie's acceptance.

Although, I must admit that I did little to heal the relationship either.

I found new ways to make a point to Elodie about my newfound happiness, with Ryon's influence bearing weight on me in the lewdest aspects. Often, Ryon and I made passionate, and sometimes loud, love in my room.

Elodie would discover us and scream about the absolute horror and dissonance I possessed. She said demons were on my back, that I was being dragged into the darkest pits of the Effluvium...just like that pernicious Order would say as well. How dare I behave in such a way?

I didn't dare tell her about my time with Yeshua and Gisela.

Ryon and I rode on this wave of enjoyment and amusement, at least until Marietta asked us to stop. She was right to ask us; I am sure the stress was not good for the baby.

So, we moved our escapades to midnight.

At first, we took long nights outside, lying in Ryon's old buggy and kissing beneath the stars. Ryon returned the horse to his father, but we kept the buggy for posterity's sake. It was where we met, where we first kissed; I didn't want to get rid of it.

But as winter arrived with a snowy vengeance, our late-night romance shifted to the basement deep beneath the house. We nestled together in a pile of blankets behind the counter, where Ryon told me about his day, and we memorized each other's bodies.

"Ms. Heartz says that her brother read through the memos at least three times now. He hasn't told her what he uncovered about the Utopia Project, though," Ryon whispered as he unlaced my dress, his fingers tracing my collarbone and down the curves of my breast.

"I get you want to know ever so badly," I said between breaths, moaning as he kissed my neck. His beard tickled, sending chills through my body. "I do too."

"Politics are so slow."

"We're at the whim of all these damn Order puppets..."

"Mhm." He grunted.

"You're just impatient!" I poked his nose.

"Are you worried?"

"Of course, I am! But these things take time."

"We've already lost the Black Market! People died!" Ryon gripped the blankets beside me. "I'm so sick of not knowing!"

"Ryon, love, please." I took his hands in mine. "Do not do anything rash. The truth will come to light. We must find our way to help kindle the flame."

"I never said I would do anything. Small acts of rebellion, right?" He smiled.

"Yes. Small acts."

We made love. It never got old. I loved the way he pulled me on his lap, the way his skin felt beneath my fingers, and the way he sank into my embrace. With experience, he got better, more confident, and even a tad cocky. I wanted to keep him against my chest forever, letting him kiss every bare bit of skin while his breaths touched the corners of my lips.

But we were more than just lovers; he had become my best friend and confidante in this short amount of time. My hero, even, but not in the traditional sense.

He didn't save me. Definitely not. But he helped me understand and see.

Wasn't that what a hero did?

We huddled on the floor by the fire as we dwindled into puttering happiness. I waited for Ryon to begin one of his usual rants about the architecture of the basement or other injustices in the city. He didn't. Instead, his eyes grew heavy, and he pulled me closer.

"What's wrong?" I asked.

"I feel...helpless," he whispered. "You heard these stories of heroes and heroines, and you think you can be like them. But...we're just small. Insignificant. Like...ants in an anthill. I'm not as big as a barn, Nanette—otherwise, people would see me!"

I restrained a laugh.

"And you...you are my sunset, but the guards just see you as a fire to extinguish. We're all at their whim...so what does it matter?" He sighed. "I shouldn't be going on like this; I should try to keep my head up. Things are being amazing. After all..." He glanced at me. "I met you."

I kissed him. Of course, I knew what Ryon meant. I often felt the same way when I worked for Captain Oberland. When we first started seeing each other, Ryon commented on my participation in the government; now, he understood where the uncertainties lay.

It was difficult to rebel when eyes watched your every movement.

We lay there as the fire dwindled, wrapped in each other's arms. My mind wandered, though. The past few weeks, I'd fallen into a nonchalant rhythm, hardly leaving the house, dreading the sight of the charred alley where the storytellers used to preach. Once when I passed it with Ryon, I broke down, and he had to hire a cabby to take us home.

There had to be a place where storytellers could speak easy and unafraid. A place hidden from the Guards, a place where smiles faced no discrimination.

I untangled myself from Ryon's arms and rose, peering around the basement. A white cloth covered an old bar, with stools piled in a corner. Dim lights hunt against the wall. There were no windows, with the only light coming from the stairway. I imagined the people that used to gather here in the tavern, laughing and drinking, singing songs and dancing, huddling together, and telling...

My eyes widened. What else did you hear about in taverns but of bar songs and legends? How many drunken bastards told fallacies to eager listeners?

Father always said people came alive in the taverns. He used to tell me a tale as a young lad, where he met my mother while listening to a story of wild beasts in the swamp.

Tales.

Stories.

Taverns proved to be safe, warm places where people gathered for a drink and a song. The storytellers needed someplace safe. Someplace no one would look.

Like the basement of a quiet home on the outskirts of the city.

I turned back to Ryon.

"Nanette? What is it?" He sat up slightly.

"You said this was a tavern once, right?"

"Based on the construction, yes, it seems so."

I knelt before him, taking both his hands and squeezing them. "I think I have an idea."

Of course, ideas often are harder to implement. In my head, it was a simple plan: convert the basement back into its glory days, where storytellers might prosper with drinks and tales.

In reality, it was harder than I ever fathomed.

First, I would have to renovate the basement without Elodie noticing.

Then I would have to sneak a bunch of people into the house without her hearing.

Then, I'd have to find storytellers without catching the attention of the Guard.

Ryon reiterated these concerns, and when I thought he was going to be the voice of reason, he pulled me close and said it was a brilliant idea.

We made love for the rest of the evening, enamored with excitement. By the time the morning came, grogginess lured us back upstairs, where our smiles painted our lips.

I spent the next few days taking inventory of everything in the basement. I didn't mind hiding down there, despite how cold it grew when the furnace rested. The constant movement and action gave me a purpose...and a reason to escape Elodie.

Whoever lived in this building before Marietta and Elodie left almost everything: a bar, a box of glasses, aged liquors, stools, tables—even napkins! It was perfect! We had everything! It was a blessing, in a way.

But it left me wondering about the story of the building as well. What happened here? How did Marietta afford such a wonderful home? Ryon intended to peruse the state records, but Jaida kept him busy almost every day. It was best we stayed low, really. The last thing we needed was for the Guard to catch a whiff of our plans.

So, we kept our heads down, trying not to draw any unnecessary attention to ourselves. As far as it concerned the Guard, we were just two young lovers, toying around in undeserving places.

One day, when I thought I was alone, I ventured into the basement and began setting up the chairs, my mind wandering. I couldn't wait to see the tavern open to storytellers galore. Already, after about a week of work, the basement had begun to resemble a tavern. With a bit more décor, the next step entered our vision: patrons and alcohol.

The creaking of the stairs pulled me from my reverie.

I paused.

Marietta stood at the bottom of the stairs with her arms crossed as she peered around the room.

"I knew you and Ryon were up to something..." Marietta stated.

"Marietta!" I jumped. "What are you doing home?"

"I took today off. Elodie is not quite well."

"Oh."

Marietta circled the room, running her fingers along the dusty glasses. She held her fingers up to the light to get a glimpse at the dirt, then frowned, her gaze caught in a distant reverie. "I remember all this..."

"I...I'm sorry?"

"My grandfather ran this tavern when I was a child. I used to play here all the time and pretend I was a barmaid. That's how I ended up in this place. My parents didn't want it, neither did my siblings...so it became my responsibility. It was falling apart when I arrived, though, so I closed it down." Marietta eyed me. "What are you planning, Nanette? This isn't *your* home."

I squirmed, turning away from her. "We just wanted to see what it looked like. That's all." The lie tasted bitter on my tongue.

"Don't lie."

"I'm not—"

"I can read you like a book. You're just like Elodie." Marietta remained calm. "This has to do with the explosion in the alleyway, doesn't it?"

I stared at the ground.

"Nanette, please tell me, what are you doing down there?"

I gathered my words. "I just wanted to listen to stories..."

Marietta's face softened. "Don't we all?"

Sometimes, I often wondered how a woman as unselfish and kind as Marietta fell in love with my abrasive sister. But, I suppose, only someone as selfless as Marietta *could* fall in love with her. Anyone else would have grown hollow and cold.

"The storytellers didn't cause the explosion..." I whispered, "The Guard—"

Marietta shook her head. "I saw the expense report. The Guard purchased an excessive amount of gunpowder recently. While it may be for their war in the north, it seemed far more than usual. I never imagined they would use it to attack their own people." Marietta sighed. "Storytellers do not harm anyone. They help examine the world and let us explore the human condition. Without them, I might not have found myself."

"Really?" I rested on a stool.

"Yes. My grandfather used to have storytellers and musicians perform in this tavern. I would gather beneath the tables to listen. I learned from them how I could be whoever I wanted. But ever since the Order worked its hands into the government, people haven't liked stories. Perhaps because stories get people to think. To learn. And...people forgot the joy the stories brought to them..." She picked a glass up and held it to the light. "I don't know for certain, but I think it was when the 'No Storytelling Statute' became law did the tavern grow quiet. My parents never said so...it happened when I was young...but it's just a guess..."

I followed her gaze around the room.

A twinge of hope twinkled in her eye for a moment, then vanished, "It is quite a shame, really, that stories have gone extinct."

"They don't have to be gone. We can bring this place back to its former glory. Imagine the stories..." I motioned to the tavern.

"Elodie won't like this."

"Elodie doesn't have to know."

"And neither do I." Marietta turned back to the stairs. "If anyone asks, I don't come into the basement. There is nothing for me here. So, as far as I'm concerned, the sheets and blankets still cover everything."

"I understand."

Marietta nodded once, then paused as she climbed up the stairs. She took one final glance over the room, her eyes narrow. "You know, my grandfather built this tavern so it would border a Witch Tunnel."

"A Witch Tunnel?" With everything Ryon ever told me about architecture and history, he never mentioned a Witch Tunnel to me!

"Few people know about them. But my grandfather told me about them. Back when the Order first outlawed magic, a bunch of those with magic built out a tunnel system so they could escape the city." She eyed the cobweb-riddled shelf behind the bar. "If I remember correctly, that's not an original shelf."

I glanced at the shelf, then back at Marietta. She already vanished through the door, leaving her blessing hanging in the air like a gentle breeze.

Once all was quiet, I raced over to the shelf to examine it. The wood was far more polished and precise than the surrounding fixtures. The construction was rigid and heavy. I was sure Ryon could examine it for hours.

I dragged my fingers along the shelving until I reached a rusted hinge against the wall. Against the side of the shelf, an indent for my fingers waited. I stuck my hand inside and pulled.

My heart thudded as I pried the shelf from the wall.

And with ease, it swung open.

Behind it, just as Marietta said, lived a dark tunnel without a single drop of light.

THIRTEEN

.---- ...--

I waited until Ryon got home to explore the Witch Tunnel. For hours, I paced back and forth, waiting for him to return. Usually, time passed in haste, but that day, the afternoon stretched out like the tunnel before me. A few times, I even considered asking Marietta to explore it with me.

But that wouldn't be the wisest move.

So I mulled about in my impatient excitement until Ryon arrived home at his usual time.

He peaked in from the top of the stairs. "Nan? You down here?"

"Ryon! About time!" I raced over to him. "I've been waiting all afternoon!"

"Yeah? I come home at the same time every day, silly." He leaned in to kiss me.

"Wait." I held up my hand. "You'll kiss me harder in a minute."

Ryon raised his eyebrows but questioned nothing as I led him over to the shelving. Once again, I pried at the hinges.

"Nanette! What are you doing?!"

I didn't answer, allowing the door to swing open. Ryon gasped.

"Marietta told me about these. Think it will be of use?" I glanced back at Ryon.

"It's a Witch Tunnel!" Ryon beamed. "I told you about these, right?"

"I don't think you did."

"Or you ignored me," Ryon said as he stroked the door frame. "I never thought I would see one. I thought it was a myth."

"It's amazing."

"But...where does it go?"

"I don't know. I was waiting for you to get home to find out."

Ryon grinned, that silly cocky grin that made my heart flutter, then leaned in for a kiss again. This time, I allowed it. As I expected, it embellished me with more excitement and passion as he lifted me up and perched me on the counter. Our lips lingered for a moment, yearning for more as our desires flourished.

I nuzzled my nose into his neck. "We should go explore before it gets too dark. We have all night for our fun."

Ryon grunted, kissed me one more time, then helped me off the counter.

Before venturing down the tunnel, I grabbed the lantern off the wall and locked the door to the cellar. Just in case, Elodie took a gander downstairs. She'd assume Ryon and I were making love, and in a fluster storm off, only to yell at us later. I'd rather she assume that than discover the truth.

Then, hands gripped tight, we approached the Witch Tunnel. Where did it go? Would we end up lost?

Or was this just our next great adventure?

Ryon, with his mind filled with architectural facts and nonsense, had an instant hunch.

"I can't believe I'm about to go into a Witch Tunnel!" He laughed, giddy as we stepped towards it. His fingers remained laced around my wrist. "You know how there isn't much magic anymore? Like there are parlor tricks and such with the storytellers. But mostly, it's gone, right? Well, that was the first thing the Order got rid of, about a hundred or something years ago. It's not a secret or anything. They actually keep it in the history books and everything. What they don't talk about is how those with magic created these tunnels to escape persecution based on some old legends or something. It's just so interesting!" Ryon tapped the stone and frowned. "Imagine the stories these tunnels hold, Nanette! We could find out what happened to all the magic and—"

"One miracle at a time." I smiled at him. "Right now, let's go save some stories."

Ryon squeezed me as he continued, "Maybe if the storytellers feel safe, then magic will come out of the shadows too! Imagine what some of them would do if given the opportunity!"

"Perhaps." While magic had been far more prominent in Stilette, we had long accepted it as something on the verge of extinction. People lost interest in spells and enchantments. Apothecaries relied more on science, performers relied more on parlor tricks; and even most with magic treated it like a joke. Yes, there were cities far away where magic continued its reign.

But not here.

Right now, we had to focus on saving the stories...before we only knew the state-sanctioned tales and nothing else.

We began our adventure down the Witch Tunnel. My heart hung heavy in my chest. Part of me yearned to tell Elodie the truth. But she wouldn't understand.

Besides, this home belonged to Marietta in the end, not Elodie. Marietta gave her blessing.

I wasn't doing anything wrong!

I shook away the fear as Ryon and I ventured further. On the surface, there wasn't anything interesting about the tunnel. Pipes creaked along the side while old gas lamps rocked back and forth above our heads. Rats scurried past us. Water dripped.

We arrived at a fork in the path. Not wanting to let go of each other, we ventured to the right, following along in silence. I tried to keep my paranoia at bay. But what if the tunnels collapsed? What if the guard were waiting for us? What if we didn't find our way back?

I clutched Ryon's arm for reassurance.

When the second tunnel branched off, we stuck to our gut and headed right again. If we stayed to the right, it would be easier to get back. After all, we had all the time in the world to explore other paths! This was an entire network, filled with hidden nooks and crannies beyond our wildest dreams! It was amazing no one else was down here! Did the Guard close off these tunnels? Or did people just stop using them?

My worries continued. What if all the tunnels exited in private residences? What if we ended up walking into someone's bedroom?

"The thing is, if we keep going right, in theory, we should end up in the countryside," Ryon muttered, almost seeming to read my thoughts. "There's gotta be an exit by some train tracks or road or something that they would have used to get outta here..."

"But there are so many tunnels. It's like a maze..." I replied.

"To confuse the Guard."

We walked for a bit longer, ducking under cobwebs and coughing at the scent of sewage. Ryon walked undeterred, the smell nothing worse than his time on the farm. He offered me his coat to cover my nose, and after gagging, I accepted.

I don't know how long we walked, but the tunnel eventually ended in a cylindrical room. No door or stairwell waited for us.

Only stone.

"Well shit... there's no ladder." Ryon pointed to the door on the ceiling.

I tilted the lantern towards the ceiling. A doorway to the surface cackled back at us.

"I bet the Order took it. Wanted no one to escape or something..." Ryon crossed his arms and sighed. "Guess we better turn back. We can check the other passages."

Ryon babbled onwards, but my attention drifted from the doorway to the wall. Curiosity struck me as I circled the room, holding up the lamps, illuminating the odd-shaped grooves on the wall. They formed a pattern of some sort, composed of different lines and dots.

"Ryon, wait," I murmured. "This looks like the tap-code I used at work for telegraphs and such..."

I pointed out the pattern. He stared at it for a moment, furrowed his brow, then smiled. "You can translate it then?"

I nodded.

"What does it say, though?"

"Let's see..."

... .--. . .- -.- . .- ... -.--

I squinted at the pattern. "That's an 'S'... 'P'..." I continued mumbling to myself, catching each letter, before saying the word aloud, "*Speakeasy.*"

As if triggered by the word, magic unraveled. The grooves shifted and pulled outwards.

And around us, the wall transformed into a spiral staircase leading up towards the ceiling. Magic might have gone into hiding, but hints remained. If you found the right words, the right stories, then even magic might flourish again.

Ryon laughed, "Nanette! You're brilliant!"

"Well, maybe we should discover where this goes before we celebrate." I held out my hand to Ryon. Together, we ascended the stairs, taking each step with care to make sure we didn't fall.

To our relief, the door unlocked from inside the tunnel. We turned the knob, and with a tad bit of elbow grease, it creaked open.

The brisk evening air stroked our faces as we crawled out into a vacant field. The Capitol glistened in the distance, lights permeating across the landscape, a constant beacon of discontent. But, out here, there were no guards. Only a quiet road, hidden by trees.

"This is perfect." Ryon smiled at me. "We found a way to get them in without being seen!"

I nodded. "It's a bit far from the city, though."

"I'm sure there are a few more entrances. We'll have to see where they lead, but at least this means at least no one will witness the coming and going from our tavern. No one will really know where it is or anything if it's all underground!

"Including Elodie."

"Especially Elodie."

Another pang of guilt hit me in the stomach upon speaking my sister's name. *I should tell her,* I thought. But I couldn't trust her. It put too much at risk.

I pulled Ryon's coat tighter around my shoulders, my heart racing with excitement, while my head pounded with thoughts and plans. There was so much to get done.

But we figured out one step.

The next part required more stealth, though: we needed patrons.

FOURTEEN

.- - - - ....-

Ryon and I continued to explore the tunnels at night. We discovered each tunnel entrance had a different tap-code word:

..-. .-. . .

Free.

-- .- --. .. -.-.

Magic.

And many more.

Ryon and I committed each path to memory, creating a pathway of broken glass along the floor to guide us back to our tavern.

During the day, I focused on cleaning the tavern and preparing for our patrons. Once, when Elodie asked what I was doing, I told her I was busy cleaning. It was a partial truth. I *was* cleaning out the cellar and organizing everything, after all.

Every day, I longed to tell everyone about my work in the tavern.

Unlike my sister, I knew how to keep my mouth shut.

So, of course, I was more than just excited when Jaida paid us a visit. I took her by both hands and led her into the empty tavern, watching as her face ignited with delight. She marveled at the progress, circling the room, stroking her fingers along the golden surfaces and décor.

"This will make a wonderful tavern," Jaida said. I didn't tell her the full goal of the space; for now, the tunnels would stay secret, guarded by our newfound collection of alcohol and brews.

But Jaida didn't come that day to talk about our silly tavern. She sat Ryon and me down at the table and sighed, a fogginess in her stares as she poured herself a drink.

"What's wrong, Jaida?" I asked.

"The Senate will vote on whether to expand the Utopia Project tomorrow. I have not heard from my brother since I showed him the Pit last week." Jaida played with her glass of whiskey. "He was absolutely heartbroken. I swear, I saw all the life leave his eyes when he saw it. He locked himself away in his chambers afterward. He hasn't taken a single visitor. Calvin is not like that at all in most cases." She glanced at Ryon and me. "I would have asked you two to accompany me, but it seemed... risky."

"I remember when you and Senator Heartz got back," Ryon mumbled, "I was expecting him to have a lot of questions for me... but he never stopped by."

"His heart was close to collapse, I think." Jaida sighed. "He spoke with me today, though. He is going to persuade the swing votes in the Senate tomorrow to vote on postponement. I am sure he wants to show the desolation to more members before it is too late."

"What do you think will happen if he can get the votes?" I asked.

"Hopefully, the wall will fall."

Ryon's eyes illuminated. "And hopefully stories can return!"

"One victory at a time, Mr. Barnes."

"Don't you want stories again, Ms. Heartz?"

"Of course I do, but it takes time, and I would rather no one gets hurt."

"Is there anything we can do to help?" I asked.

"Oh, no, not right now. No. Just...keep to your duties..." Jaida furrowed her brow, then beamed, "You two have quite the set up here, though! When do you intend to open to the public? I am sure this will be a wonderful addition to the Capitol!"

And with that, the subject changed. Period.

I glanced at Ryon. "We hope to open soon. We need to get the word out..."

"And quietly at that," Ryon added.

Jaida narrowed her eyes, calculating our intentions, then gasped, "You're opening a speakeasy!"

There was that word again. *Speakeasy.*

Ryon interjected in haste, "We're not operating an illegal bar."

"Come now. Why else would you need to gather patrons quietly?" Jaida wiggled her eyebrows. "You can tell me. We trust each other, right?"

I responded, careful with each word, reflecting upon the events from the earlier weeks, "Stories don't die in flames. They need somewhere else to prosper."

"That they do..." Jaida agreed, "But please, be careful, both of you. I do not want to lose my friends and companions. It would break my heart."

Jaida helped us acquire the proper permits to sell alcohol and run the tavern as a barrier of protection against the guard. This left Ryon with the task of venturing to his village to acquire barrels of cheap liquor from his uncle's brewery. He loaded the barrels onto his buggy and carted them to Elodie's house deep in the middle of the night. His uncle was exuberant to help, though we kept most of the details to a minimum while we worked. While he did the heavy labor, he left me with the impossible: inform storytellers of their new sanctuary... without being caught.

During the day, while Ryon worked for Jaida, I ventured into the city. The cold autumn air ate at my skin, sending chills through my body as I walked, despite my three coats and two scarves. Snow flurries decorated the air, dancing with the frigid gusts of wind. In the back of a buggy, the wind felt like daggers. As I walked through town, it reminded me of screams.

I longed for the tepid humidity of Volfium's swamps.

At every block, I ducked into the shops or restaurants to bask in a moment of warmth. I have to admit, I didn't have a plan. Ryon and I had debated for hours the nights prior: what if we posted flyers, or checked the old alleyway, or asked Jaida? Nothing seemed right. Everything had the potential to lead back to the Guard.

In the end, we came up with one clear decision: word-of-mouth was the best choice. If we found a familiar storyteller and let them spread the news, then our little tavern may grow organically.

But where could I find a storyteller in the day-to-day of the Capitol?

Had any even survived?

I survived. Surely others did as well, hiding now in the shadows, whispering their stories and performing slights-of-hand.

It was odd walking past the alleyway, charred and crisp, where weeks earlier, I nearly died. It stood now, vacant and burned, with two guards standing at the entrance. A few people passed by, stealing a glance, before being hurried along by the guards. I kept my head bowed, peering for but a second. Did the guards even know what they defended? Were they aloof, like Captain Oberland? Or brainwashed by someone like Captain Cordova?

I didn't look up as I entered the plaza. My first thought was I could people watch and seek someone I knew in the crowd until Ryon left for work. Perhaps he would be braver in approaching the storytellers; he was outgoing and talkative and knew a friendly face when he saw one. Me? I was just a girl from Volfium. I hadn't even been in Rosada for a year yet! While my Rosadian was impeccable, I still punctuated certain phrases in a way that caused people to pause.

Plus, I didn't bear the same confidence as Ryon or even Elodie. I had always valued a quiet life, but now I rode on the edge of a rebellion. This was more than I ever fathomed!

I settled onto the bench and peered around the plaza. With the birth of the new year arriving in the next few days, the square bustled with activity. Vendors sold different Year Glasses, bejeweled with countless gems, while others sold equally glamorous outfits. The Temple gazed down upon it all with a glint in its windows, welcoming the droves of individuals heading inside for service. I scoffed to myself. Didn't people know that the Brothers and Sisters of the Order told preposterous stories?

At least the stories told in alleyways were fun.

Stories.

Yet, I struggled to pull my gaze away from the Temple. I hated everything that the Order of the Effluvium stood for, but an idea led me towards its doors.

Storytellers do not just create stories; they absorb them. Inevitably, they would flock to the one place where stories still lingered.

The Temple.

I loathed every minute I spent in the Temple. I ignored the preaching, the hymns, and the prayers, allowing their words to fly over my head. They blessed the arriving new year, made promises to the Effluvium while dictating another year of orderly reign. But did I pray? No. Did I absorb what they said? Absolutely not.

It didn't matter to me.

It was all just a story.

And not a good one at that.

I kept my attention instead on the congregation. The storytellers had to be here. I knew it.

I have learned over the years that a few telltale signs exist of storytellers. They sit eagerly, they hang on every word, and they will describe their day with such detail that you can almost see the events play out before you. While I couldn't ask people to talk that day, I still observed. The religious types bowed their heads. The children fidgeted in their seats, but a few hung onto every word as if calculating and gathering them for a repertoire of stories.

And after watching them for a bit, I recognized quite a few from the Black Market. They used to perform stories or slights-of-hand there. An old woman told us the story about the Forest Queen. A man performed magic tricks, and another sang with a voice so pure it might have belonged to the sky.

But here, in the Temple, dressed in drab colors, they could have been anyone.

I suppose that's the true nature of storytellers. They're like everyone and everywhere. That must be why the Order fears them. They hide in the streets. They speak without fear. It'd be impossible to cut out everyone's tongue.

They would try, without a doubt.

I waited in the back as the congregation filed out of the Temple. Elodie walked among them. I dropped my head down, hiding my face with my hair. She walked straight past me. It was strange seeing her; at home, she always had a snarl on her lips, a glare in her eyes. Here, she looked tired, carrying the weight of pregnancy on her back. Part of me wanted to reach out to her, tell her I wanted to talk; perhaps I could be her companion during her restless nights, tell her stories, and laugh until sleep became the champion.

But we were nothing more than strangers.

Had I ever even known my sister?

I didn't dwell on it, redirecting my attention as Elodie left to the storytellers striding towards me.

Within an instant, I locked gazes with the old woman.

"Oh!" the woman whispered and reached for my hands. "You're okay! I wasn't sure...the explosion..."

"I'm fine. How are you, though?" I asked in a hushed tone.

"I prevail."

"But without a haven, yes?"

"We will find another..." The woman's eyes grew heavy. "For now, our voices will continue with the softness of moonbeams in the daytime."

"You do not need to wait for a clear night. There is no reason we can't...speak easy somewhere else." I glanced over my shoulder to make sure no one listened. "Tell the others. There's a new place where stories can reign...and I hold the key."

FIFTEEN

．－ － － ．．．．．

That evening, and all the next day, Ryon and I prepared for our Grand Opening. We planned little, outside of basic security measures, to prevent Elodie from discovering our little secret. All we hoped, really, was that the storytellers arrived at the right tunnel without arousing suspicion. I told them to go to the tunnel with the tap code "speak easy" for the first night. We had already prepared the stairway for them in the tunnels. We decided that each night, only one tunnel would offer entrance into our bar. Other than that, what else could we plan? Already, I told the storytellers to whisper when they entered, but even that didn't concern us much.

The house was soundproof.

When Elodie wasn't home, one of us banged pots in the basement while the other positioned themselves in the different bedrooms to check the noise.

Was it magic? Or good construction? I wasn't sure.

I knew this: it was a perfect secret bar.

Yet I did harbor some guilt for doing this right under my sister's nose. She had been kind enough to take me in after our father died. Then I went and fell in love with a man she despised, got myself hurt in an illegal Black Market, and set up this speakeasy right below her house. But what was more important? My sister or people's lives?

An internal battle waged over my morals. My parents raised me on two core principles: family and righteousness. This time, the two principles clashed. The nights leading up to our Grand Opening, I trembled, tossing and turning through my nightmares. Ryon would pull me close, promise he was by my side, and tell me this conflict was normal.

Now, with the Grand Opening upon us, there was no turning back. It was now or never.

We spent that evening wiping the glasses, setting the tables, and scattering a few lanterns around the small wooden stage. At the top of the stairs, Ryon installed a contraption of pots and pans that would alert us of any unwelcome arrivals. If someone dared even touch the front or back doors, it would tug at a string beneath the floorboards, sending a marble toppling down the pots and pans...

Clank.

Clank.

Clank.

We heard them over loud music, and hopefully, that warning would give us enough time to usher the storytellers away.

We didn't care if that woke Elodie and Marietta. If the Guard came, the Speakeasy's life ended.

"You ready?" Ryon grinned at me as I tested the warning system one last time. He wore his finest suit, his red curls slicked back, his beard trimmed. I synched my waist for this occasion, twirling in my long blue skirt. We looked posh and sophisticated and ready to welcome our new guests.

I glanced at Ryon. "I'm scared."

"Me too." He kept grinning. "I think that's expected."

Once we were certain Elodie had gone to bed, Ryon unhinged the shelves leading into the tunnels and lit a blue flame outside the tavern. The advert we gave to the few storytellers was simple.

If the blue flame is present, walk ten minutes north, where the fields are empty, and the cows are plenty. There, the ground will welcome you, and if you head straight, you'll find freedom at last.

I watched from the doorway as the blue light captured Ryon's face. His smile warmed me. How did I end up with such a handsome man? His hazel eyes always glistened, his freckles like stardust on his cheeks. I really was lucky.

And he made the night easier.

We sat by the bar, awaiting our first storyteller. I kept checking out the cellar window, occasionally stealing a glance at the few people walking down the road.

No one came to our tavern as the moon rose high and the stars bejeweled the sky.

No visitors. No storytellers. No one.

Just a gentle mist humming across the lawn.

With every passing hour, my heart grew heavier. Perhaps this was a pipe dream after all; why would anyone dare come to a mysterious house on the edge of town? We could easily be spies for the Guard looking to abolish more storytellers. For all they knew, the Guard captured and brainwashed me.

I probably wouldn't have come either.

After a time, I ventured onto the porch and stared out across the field. Ryon brought two glasses of whiskey, and we sat there in silence, nursing our drinks, watching as the moon fell and the sun captured the edge of the road. Red painted the clouds.

As the roosters crowed, Ryon turned off the lantern while I cleaned downstairs. I didn't say a word as we put the canvas back over the bar and tables. In a mere instant, our dream of a little storytelling bar became nothing more than that: a dream. This really was just a basement beneath my sister's house.

I shouldn't have thought of it as anything else.

I lay in bed all day, drifting in and out of sleep, my head pressed to Ryon's arm. He said nothing. We both thought the same thing.

Failure.

Perhaps it was for the best, though. I didn't need to dig a deeper moat between Elodie and me. Marietta didn't need to be involved, either. Ryon wouldn't have another reason to be, for lack of a better word, on Elodie's shit-list. It was best for me to move past this petty dream.

Ryon eventually got out of bed, kissing my forehead and leaving me alone. I listened as he bickered with Elodie in the hallway. I pictured it: the two of them, standing face-to-face, glowering. My dearest Ryon, who wore friendliness on his sleeve, had fallen prey to hatred. Why? Why couldn't they get along with each other?

I pulled the duvet to my chin. My lip quivered. I was just cold, I told myself. I wasn't sad. Shouldn't I have known this would not work? It had been a stupid, silly idea.

It would have been better to put my energy into finding our own place.

Hours passed. Ryon came in and out of the room, bringing me tea and food, soothing my worries, and promising he was still here. Usually, on our days off like this, we would go into the city together. He was growing stir crazy, pacing around the room. But my sweet Ryon didn't pressure me to get up, letting me wallow in self-pity.

It was what I needed.

Elodie's voice in the hallway tugged me out of my woes, though. This time, I heard her clear as day, standing right outside my door.

Ryon's shuffling greeted her outside my door.

"What have you done to my sister? I haven't seen her all day!" Elodie barked.

"She's not feeling well," Ryon grumbled.

"You kept her up late, didn't you? Repulsive! You pervert!"

I sat up slightly, fury riding in my chest.

"What?" Ryon said.

"She needs rest! Get out of here—and stop bringing her these sugar-filled pastries! They're probably what made her sick in the first place!" A plate clattered to the floor.

I imagined Ryon standing there, his back tense, and the lump in his throat moving with a single gulp. He probably clenched his hands, as he always did when angry, while keeping his tone level. "Your sister is an adult."

"You've tarnished her!"

"I did no such thing!"

"She was my best friend before you came!"

"Really? Then why don't you listen to what she has to say?"

Thud.

Crash.

I shot up out of bed and raced to the door, throwing it open.

Ryon knelt on the floor, holding his head between his knees. A picture lay shattered on the ground beside him. Elodie glared.

"I suppose you aren't as strong as you look." Elodie spat, crossing her arms over her chest.

"ELODIE! How could you!?" I raced to Ryon's side. Blood streamed from the side of his face.

"I'm fine," Ryon reassured me.

My fury remained transfixed on Elodie. "Why can't you get along with him?"

"Why couldn't you find someone respectable?" she shouted at me.

"Ryon is respectable!"

"He knows nothing, Nanette! He spews lies!"

"They're not lies! I've seen what happened!"

"Oh, Nanette! Mr. Barnes has brainwashed you. You have seen nothing."

"I saw the Pit!" I wanted to scream, but I kept my voice level. "I saw them drag innocent people into slavery!"

"No, you haven't."

"I have! I can show you!"

"Do not waste my time." Elodie turned away. "That is preposterous!"

Before I responded, Marietta stormed upstairs. "What is going on up here?"

Neither Elodie nor I spoke.

"Quiet, both of you!" Marietta's gaze softened on Ryon's face. "What happened? Oh, you poor boy." She raced over to Ryon and helped him stand. "Let's get you cleaned up now. That is a deep cut."

I rose from my spot to follow.

Marietta stopped me. "Nanette. I think it is best you stay in your room." She glared at Elodie. "You too. You need to rest and shouldn't be bickering with your sister."

"But—" Elodie and I spoke at the same time.

"No. Room. Now."

I frowned in Ryon's direction, then slumped back into my bedroom. Marietta would make a wonderful mother someday if she could boss around two adult women without flinching.

I woke again to Ryon brushing my hair back, a smile on his face. Marietta patched the cut on his head, and other than walking with a bit of sway, as well as a blackening bruise around his eye, he seemed otherwise fine.

"Nanette," he whispered.

I took his hand and kissed between his knuckles. "Hi."

"Do you want to try again?"

"Try what?" I blinked.

"The Speakeasy?"

"No one showed up last night..." I stared towards the window. "Is it really worth trying again? Imagine Elodie's wrath if she found out? If she hurt you like that after a mere argument—"

"Marietta has our back." Ryon sat on the bed. "She made a good point while cleaning me up today. You know, people might've come by...but as scouts. We saw a few people in the street. Maybe they were scouts or something trying to see if we had Guards stationed outside. They might come by tonight."

"Maybe..." I didn't feel hopeful.

"C'mon, let's try one more time. If it doesn't work... Marietta said that we can sell all the stuff in the basement and use the proceeds to find a place of our own."

"And if it does? Then what?" I met his gaze.

"Then we have ourselves a fancy Speakeasy."

My confidence wavered, but I followed Ryon down the stairs, anyway. I kept a hand on his arm as he stumbled, his sense of balance not quite right. He remained optimistic, despite everything, wearing a dapper suit. He let his curls hang loose this time, though, his beard a little more shaggy than last night.

I didn't dress to impress this time, sitting instead in my beige linen dress at a table, watching as night ascended through the cellar window. Ryon sat beside me, squeezing me tight.

"Be hopeful, okay?" He grinned at me.

I returned his infectious smile.

We sat there for a couple of hours. No one knocked.

Like my heart, the tavern remained empty.

And with each passing moment, my last few shreds of hope dwindled.

Until a knock echoed from behind the bar.

Ryon and I both jumped.

"Do you think..." Words failed me.

Ryon raced over to open it. A small group stood right there in the Witch Tunnel, staring past Ryon at me.

I recognized the woman at the front of the group; she was the same woman from the Temple.

"Is this... are we welcome here?" The woman whispered.

I stared at her, then at Ryon, who greeted her with haste.

"Of course you are!" Ryon exclaimed. "Come... come in! We've been waiting for you!"

It was everything I ever dreamed.

And more.

The three storytellers who arrived accepted warm cups of cocoa, as well as liquor, before situating themselves in different corners of the room. Ryon knew the two men and chatted away with them while I sat beside the old woman. But unlike Ryon, I didn't speak.

I didn't know what to say.

My nerves rose like a storm inside my stomach, ready to take control.

The old woman smiled at me, then without a word, walked to the stage at the head of the room. With a single beat, she wove a tale.

Our small tavern fell silent. The old woman's tale wrapped around us, taking us on an adventure with pirates at sea. I couldn't recant the whole thing even if I tried. It would lose the luster and confidence the woman carried as she spoke. But it spoke about a siren who yearned not to be silent. She fought each man who came to take her away from home, screaming, 'I am present.'

And as the old woman told the tale, her eyes stayed locked with mine.

Once she finished her story, another storyteller took his place on the makeshift stage. The rest of the night panned out like this: someone told a story, then the next person went up to perform. Even Ryon took the stage at one point, telling a half-enchanted tale about a talking horse. He didn't quite have a knack for storytelling, but I applauded his efforts.

"You're up!" He hopped from the stage.

"Oh...I don't know if I can. I'm not really a storytell-er..." I flushed.

"Come on, Nan! If I can do it, you can too."

"Do I at least get a kiss for good luck?"

He pecked my cheek and whispered, "You'll get more after you tell a story."

I pouted at him as I approached the stage. Why was my heart pounding? I didn't know. I told stories before, but only under protection and safety. This was under the guise of breaking the rules; this wasn't only Ryon or my father or Elodie. I had an audience filled with strangers watching me.

"Um..." I stared around the room at the small crowd, recalling a story my father once told me. "Once upon a time, there was a girl who set the sky on fire. They say once that the sky was nothing but black. The girl, she said, could make it blue. They laughed at her, though. For a blue sky is but a myth. A legend. Like this story I'm telling now.

"Her passion to prove it strengthened her. Each day, she dabbled in magic, tending to the flame. Her passion grew, as did the fire, and one day, it towered above the forest. People didn't come near her. They believed her a witch destined aiming to destroy the world.

"But while her fire brought light, it also brought fear. As the plumes grew higher, the high rulers grew worried. They sent their best warriors to stop her. She saw them coming from her spot, the fire lighting their path and their weapons. The girl had to escape.

"So she coated herself in fire and soared through the sky. But the ruler's warriors did not stop. They climbed after her. They chased her around the sky, never to stop, constantly battling dark with light.

"The story goes that the Goddess of Light was born that day, while the army of darkness followed. That is why the sky is blue only part of the day. At least...that's what they say where I'm from in Stilette."

I stopped, catching my breath, and let the story resonate around the room. My throat hurt from talking.

Ryon grinned, and his eyes sparkled. Excitement knitted its way over my lips.

I did it! I told a story!

In *my* tavern!

And at least it wasn't a story about a talking horse.

SIXTEEN

.---- -....

The night passed in a blur of liquor and joy. I never laughed so much, throwing my arms around Ryon as we listened to each story, swaying to the steady beats of breathing and serenity. Somehow, we shut down the bar before Elodie awoke that morning, making our way back upstairs, only to collapse in a fit of exhaustion. The stories decorated my dreams, and when I finally woke that early afternoon, still wearing the clothes from the night before, a slight smile prickled at my lips.

Ryon snored beside me, his red hair sticking in every direction. I brushed aside his curls. "Ryon..."

He grunted.

"We did it," I whispered in his ear. "The stories are back."

"Mmm."

I poked his cheek. "C'mon. Wake up!"

"Headache," he groaned.

"You drank too much."

"I drank just enough."

"C'mon." I leaned over him, pressing my nose into his neck. "I don't want to go downstairs alone."

"Who says anything about going downstairs?" He opened one eye and smirked at me.

"Ryon, you devil!"

"We need to celebrate."

I threw myself into his arms, and we devolved into a fit of sloppy, morning-breath kisses.

We only got as far as him unlacing my bodice when Elodie's shriek from downstairs pulled us away from our cravings. My heart thudded. Did she discover our story-telling bar? Was she coming to kick us out?

Was she in labor?

Elodie screamed again.

"Want me to go see?" Ryon asked.

"No. I'll go. She's less likely to hurt me."

I pulled on my overcoat and rushed down the stairs. Marietta met me in the kitchen, exhaustion clear on her face, hair bundled in curling pins. We both sighed in unison when we found Elodie not by the cellar door but by the entranceway.

She cried out once more.

"Elodie, my love, what is it?" Marietta ran to her side. "What is it, my love?"

She pointed with a trembling finger out to the lawn.

At first, I saw nothing.

Then, I saw everything.

I froze, bile rising in my throat at the sight.

From the tree in the middle of the front yard hung a body.

And it belonged to none other than the old woman from our tavern.

Ryon and I waited on the steps for the Guard to arrive. Neither of us spoke. We both had vague memories of all the patrons leaving the tavern in hushed tones. The old woman left with them. So, what happened? How did she end up hanging from our tree?

Despite the horror, I didn't cry. Death is one of those strange things where tears often come later. I didn't cry for my mother or father when they passed until much later, nor did I feel tears now. Instead, I sank into a hollowness in the pit of my stomach, huddled against Ryon in the brisk autumn wind.

Captain Cordova arrived with an entourage of Guards. He marched past Ryon and me, paying a quick glare in my general direction and cocking one eyebrow before heading inside the house. Each of his lieutenants looked identical: slicked-back hair, dark, focused eyes, and glowers on their lips.

One man with dusty blond hair nearly kicked me as he followed his captain.

I stopped Ryon from shouting at the lieutenant, motioning him to follow me inside so we could listen. As I closed the door, I stopped for a moment, watching the cadets lower the old woman from the tree to throw her into their wagon.

They treated her like baggage. Nothing more.

No respect.

Just an object.

I shook off the anger and redirected my attention to the conversation in the kitchen, standing to the side like a mere fly on the wall.

"I don't know who she is or why she is here," Elodie bemoaned to Captain Cordova as he paced the kitchen. "We just found her outside."

"It mighta been a suicide," the lieutenant who almost kicked me said.

"Thank you for the observation, Lieutenant Reynolds," Captain Cordova grumbled.

"Why would she choose MY home, though?" Elodie asked. Marietta fidgeted beside her.

"An area of convenience, perhaps. It's far enough away from the city that no one would stop her, but by a home, so someone might find her. A cry for help? Attention? Only the Effluvium knows." The captain closed his notebook. "It is a sad thing that happens. But alas, Death comes, and we have the choice to live or mourn."

Elodie wiped her eyes. "There are plenty of other homes. Why us?"

"Why not? Why anyone? What excludes you from terrors, Ms. Lieu?"

Elodie's lips drew into a line.

Captain Cordova bowed. "Thank you for reporting this, Ms. Lieu. If anyone here remembers any details that could help our investigation, please come by the Capitol Building. Understood?"

"Thank you, Captain. We will." Marietta interjected herself in the conversation.

The captain saluted, and with his Guards, filed towards the exit. He slowed as he passed me, his voice nothing more than a hiss. "And if you think of anything, Miss Ivans, I do hope you'll speak up. I'd hate to see something happen to you."

I stiffened.

The captain stayed no longer, marching into the yard where his guards finished placing the old woman in a body bag. Without a sign of care or sympathy, the biggest guard threw the body over his shoulder, and they marched back to their buggy.

In a blink, the midday fog settled over the landscape. And the Guard had disappeared, leaving Ryon and me on the doorstep.

Silence sank into the air. I didn't need magic or need to ask how Ryon felt. Was this our fault? Would the old woman still be alive if we had just behaved?

Eventually, Elodie rose, placing her hand on her pregnant belly, and wobbled across the room to where Ryon and I stood. Her eyes pierced us, her blue eyes piercing like a sapphire, then fixated solely on Ryon. "What did you do?"

"Elodie!" Marietta clamored to her feet. "Don't accuse him of anything!"

"It was him! He's a no-good slob, and I do not want him in my house!"

"I didn't do anything!" Ryon objected.

I gripped his arm to hold him back.

"That is a load of malarkey!" Elodie gauged. "You cause trouble. I'm sure you robbed her or something, then she came to find you, and then you killed her!"

"He did no such thing!" I raised my voice. "Don't you dare accuse him of murdering someone!"

"Come on, Dor—Nanette, he's scum!"

"I was with him all night! He didn't leave my side!"

Before Elodie could shout back, Marietta held out both hands, hulking over my sister and me, her eyes dark and stern. Her voice rumbled, "Enough!"

I recoiled back into Ryon's arms.

"You two are acting like schoolgirls. An old woman has *died*, and you are bickering!" Marietta pressed her fingers to the bridge of her nose. "Elodie, my love, you shouldn't stress yourself. And Nanette, you look exhausted. Both of you must go to bed at once."

"But—" Elodie and I protested at the same time.

"NOW!"

I pivoted towards the stairs and grabbed Ryon's hand.

"Ryon, I'd like to talk with you," Marietta stopped me.

"Oh. Alright." Ryon said.

He released my fingers and smiled at me. His eyes didn't have their usual joy. I partially blamed myself. Perhaps this was all for naught.

"Go take a nap," Ryon whispered and kissed my knuckles.

Elodie gagged.

I stared at him and nodded. Then, without a word, I walked up the stairs into our bedroom.

I passed out as soon as I hit the pillow and dreamt of the old woman telling a story about pirates.

Ryon woke me at sunset. The setting sun painted the room orange, and my stomach growled from missed meals. Ryon's own hair blended with the room, and for a second, I thought he melted into the walls.

"Hi, love." He grinned at me, stroking back my hair. "Sleep well?"

"I'm hungry."

He pulled a tray over, embellished with steaming soup, fresh bread, and mashed potatoes. "I knew you would be."

I ate in silence for a few minutes, pushing the potatoes to the far side of the tray while I snacked on the bread. Once my stomach stopped trying to interrupt the conversation, I turned to Ryon. "What did Marietta want with you?"

He turned to the window. "She...has a proposition."

"A...proposition?" That wasn't what I was expecting. I expected Marietta to tell Ryon to destroy the tavern and for us to leave. I didn't foresee any bargain or, as Ryon put it, a proposition.

Ryon wiped my mouth with his handkerchief. "She wants to move Elodie into the city. She thinks it would be better for her."

Elodie loved being in the heart of it all. The city was where all the richest and most fashionable individuals lived; Elodie could walk to the Gallery and the Temple.

I couldn't imagine Marietta there, though. They didn't have that type of money...unless they sold the house.

"Oh..." I put my spoon down on the tray.

Ryon continued babbling, "She also thinks being closer will provide new opportunities for their babe and everything...and fewer expenses for cabbies and the like. I think it's ridiculous. The city is loud and bright. You don't see the stars. Great to go there during the day but to live there? No, thank you. But that's not the point. The point is Marietta needs to sell the house for this to be possible."

"Right..."

"But she made an offer. She told me that if we can squander up the savings for a down payment over the next month, she can get us a good loan from the treasury." Ryon squeezed my hands. "We can keep the house and make it ours if we want. She'll give it to us at a good rate too."

"But we only have one job between the two of us," I sighed. "I guess I can go get work somewhere as a wench or something."

"You're already a wench!" Ryon's lips parted into a wide smile.

I glared at him.

"No! I mean it! You've got yourself a tavern downstairs."

"You're not seriously saying we should keep it open... even after what happened?"

"Especially after what happened! There is no way that woman committed suicide. That was the work of someone...and whoever that was, I bet they were trying to send a message: stories are illegal. But they clearly didn't know about the tavern. They just saw a handful of storytellers out and about last night." Ryon leaned forward. "So what do we do? We show them we're not afraid. They can't prove we're telling stories. We're just a fancy little tavern, right?"

Ryon's own confidence wrapped around me. It was magic in its own way. I smiled at him. We talked about this; we spoke of the risks; people told stories knowing the possibilities. But storytelling is a human condition, and everyone has the right to speak easy.

"So, I run the bar, and you go work in the capitol? Seems like we swapped roles." I smirked at him. "What happened to my little cabby driver?"

Ryon grinned. "I stopped being a barn is what happened."

"You're not a barn anymore?"

"Nah, not at all. I'm in your arms."

His smile was contagious as always, and I pulled him close to me.

Only to have the bowl of soup clatter off the tray and spill all over the sheets.

SEVENTEEN

.---- --...

We waited until after the birth of the new year to reopen the bar. Ryon and I kept our heads low, foregoing the Year Birth Celebrations in the city center to nestle together in the quiet house while Elodie and Marietta celebrated. We spent our days plotting the future of the tavern, with our primary focus on the new security measures to protect our storytellers. We settled on one option: once we became the rightful owners of the house, we would turn the building into a traditional tavern. Regular visitors could spend the night in one of the many rooms, while those who knew the passcode could enter the basement through the tunnel system.

We kept the plan quiet, waiting to do anything to the house until Marietta and Elodie moved. For now, we relied only on our own guile and precautions to protect everyone from harm.

To keep the Guard off our trail, Ryon took the reins in finding the storytellers during his lunch breaks while I stayed at home to quell Elodie's suspicions.

Not that Elodie was around much. I had seen little of Elodie since we found the body. She either hid away in her room or ventured into the city to shop for the babe...and to look at real estate.

So more often than not, I spent the day alone, tending to the tavern, securing our alarm, and counting the days until storytellers graced the stage again.

The day before we planned to reopen, a knock interrupted my cleaning on the front door. I dropped my broom and raced upstairs to find Jaida surprising me at the front door.

"Jaida! I did not expect you!" I exclaimed.

"Nanette, darling." Jaida took both my hands. "I am so glad to see you okay."

"Why wouldn't I be?" I ushered her inside the foyer. "Please, come in!"

"I have little time, unfortunately, Nanette. I must go back to work soon. Ryon has my back, but at some point, someone will come searching for me."

"Jaida, please, stay. I—"

"Nanette, dear, please listen to me."

I slumped and stared at her.

"I one-hundred percent support you and Ryon in this crazy endeavor, but I am pleading you be careful."

"We are! We've set up this system and are keeping to a small group—"

"Yes, and I am relieved to see that. But I need you to know something."

"What is it? What's wrong?" My heart plummeted in my chest.

"The old woman found dead outside this house was no accident. She was murdered." Jaida lowered her voice. "My brother did some investigating after hearing about the murder. She was a well-known and beloved storyteller here in the Capitol."

"Yes, I know. She frequently told stories."

"And that is why they murdered her."

"Murdered?" I shook my head. It didn't surprise me; everything about the death seemed too perfect. Ryon had already voiced his suspicions. "So is it a warning? Like Ryon thought?

"Perhaps. There is much to be uncovered. The Order has its hands all throughout the government. It will stop at nothing to rid the province of storytellers and stop their magic from spreading." Jaida looked over her shoulder again. "I have a hunch based on hearsay throughout the Capitol Building. One of the Order's cronies saw the poor old woman leave the fields. Recognizing her, they beat her up and left her on a local's doorstep. This time, it was your doorstep, the house closest to the fields. If they discovered your tavern, then I'm sure they would have attacked here too."

"But that's barbaric! She was a kind, old woman."

"Yes, but she told stories, didn't she? She toyed with magic and stood against the Order. And that is all they care about." Jaida squeezed my hand. "All I'm asking is that you be careful and be aware of everyone you let into the tavern. If you let the wrong person in, then it could be the end for you or Ryon."

I nodded.

"That being said," Jaida's smile returned, "I cannot wait to see this tavern in all its glory. A true speakeasy! I never would have thought! I'll have to talk with my brother about opening one in the Newbird Region, especially if the Order's plans hinder us further."

"The Utopian Project, you mean?"

"Yes, but I think something like this would be a way to stick it to them if you catch my drift." She winked. "Although so many of the people out there are backward and nosy. It might not be as easy to hide…" Jaida glanced around the house, "It is a shame, though, that we have to resort to this."

"At least stories will survive."

"Yes, and that is all that matters." She sighed. "Well, I best be off. I shall see you tomorrow then."

"You mean, you're coming to the speakeasy? Even after everything you said? "

"Of course! My brother is as well! I wouldn't miss it for the world! Ryon has been babbling about your success... and you should see all the work he has put into getting the patrons—oh, I spoke too soon! But you'll see! You'll see!"

Before I could question anything else, she kissed my forehead like a sister would, waved me goodbye, and started down the road back to the Capitol.

"Wait! Jaida!" I raced after her.

Jaida stopped by the fence, "Nanette, I must be off."

"One last question."

"Yes?"

"Did you find out the name of the old woman? She never told anyone..." I looked at my feet, ashamed.

I never even thought to ask.

"Ah, yes. Her name was Brenda Harley."

"Brenda..." I said to myself and nodded, "Thank you."

Jaida waved, then left with haste. I watched her leave, yearning for her to stay longer. But I also reveled in the excitement of her return. The senator was coming too! I couldn't believe it!

Yet, the excitement tapered off at the thought of Old Brenda Harley, of our tavern, of the Guard, and of Ryon. He came home each night exhausted, working overtime to get this place up and running. I could only imagine one day we'd be self-sufficient. He'd gone from a farm boy to a cabby and to a tavern owner working in the government in a short time. But a constant cloud hung over me, warning that something would take him away from me. Would he have to work again for his father? Or would I have to go back to Volfium? Would Elodie kick us out of the house before she and Marietta settled in the city?

Would we end up like poor Brenda Harley?

No. Staring in the tavern, at the tables and chairs set up around the stage, I realized one thing:

We were going to win. Or go out fighting.

With daylight fizzling off with the sunset, Jaida and her brother, the notorious Senator Calvin Heartz, arrived at our tavern the following night. To tighten security, Ryon established a secret password that would change each night, along with the open tunnel location. Word-of-mouth spread it, referral-based only, and we would cap attendance each night.

We made an exception for Jaida and Calvin.

I hopped from foot to foot as Senator Heartz introduced himself to me. His wide smile glistened on his face, shining beneath his curly beard. When he laughed, his eyes lit up like Jaida's face, excitement shared between them in equal dosages.

Senator Heartz skulked around our tavern, towering over it like a giant, making me feel like an insect on the wall. He had presence, he had standing, and he spent his evening here, listening to our tales. Ryon walked by his side in pride, never shutting his mouth as if the two of them were old friends.

"You have put in much work, haven't you, Mr. Barnes?" Senator Heartz chuckled, his voice booming.

"I can't really take the credit. Nanette has put her heart in soul into this." Ryon flashed a grin in my direction.

My heart leapt.

"Yes, Miss Ivans." Senator Heartz finally acknowledged me. "Jaida has told me much about you! It is a pleasure to meet you at last."

"Same to you, Senator."

"Please, call me Calvin."

My face warmed.

Ryon chuckled, "You're embarrassing her, Senator. Please, save it for the stories."

"Oh, I'm not a storyteller. I am just here to observe."

"What about you, Jaida?" I asked.

Jaida joined her brother's laughter. "Oh no, no...I'm afraid not. I heard you told a story, though!"

"That won't be happening again..." I slumped into my chair. I didn't have the confidence or the energy to tell another tale this time. Our storytellers could be the stars.

"I don't think we'll be short of stories." Ryon leaned against the counter and yawned. "I got a word out to a few people I trust. It's a good password. No one will think of it."

"You still haven't told me what it is."

"Oh, that's easy. 'Nanette is a sunset.'"

The relaunch was a success. At least fifteen storytellers arrived throughout the night. Each one knocked thrice on the bar door, provided Ryon a coin for entry and a whisper of my name, then ventured into our secret tavern. I kept the bar stocked, putting on my fake smile and laughing as a drunken man came over, croaking about giant frogs.

Jaida and Calvin stayed for a while. I forgot how peculiar stories were for people like them. They listened to each story with intent, eyes wide and in awe. In Stilette, ridiculous tales like this bolstered in the streets. But to people like Senator Heartz and his sister, stories were legends. They never fathomed such tales, and when each one ended, they both hopped to their feet, clapping like children.

The Heartz siblings took their leave after midnight, exchanging places with a few other storytellers whispering on the bar stools. I served them their liquor, then leaned against the back counter. Storytellers gathered in a hushed group while an elderly man told a tale on the stage. A few practiced magic parlor tricks. Yet, I couldn't help but feel, despite the wonderful turnout, that the speakeasy still felt empty. This place needed an audience. It needed a reason to be boisterous.

And it couldn't start jeering until Elodie moved out.

Ryon joined me as the tavern dwindled to sleep. We had instructed each storyteller to take a different path out of the tunnels, hindering the possibility of discovery. No guards came, to our relief. Even after the last storyteller disappeared, Ryon continued standing alert on the porch for another thirty minutes before helping me clean the mess in the tavern.

His smile punctuated his cheeks with dimples. "That went well, I think."

"It did." I agreed. "Let's hope we don't get another warning on our lawn."

"I don't think we will. We were cautious. People left in intervals. No one was watching. I even circled the perimeter a few times." He nodded to himself. "Besides, if they knew about us, wouldn't they have snagged the people in charge? Or stormed in or something?"

He was right. Yet my worries remained heavy in my chest. What if they came knocking in the morning? What if Elodie discovered us?

Gently, Ryon nudged my chin. "Don't worry, alright? We did it. This time for real. Once we get this thing into being a real tavern, no one's gonna notice us. We'll just be in another place on the outskirts of town. Who cares about a bunch of poor old tavern owners?"

"We're not *old*." I giggled.

"Speak for yourself. I feel ancient."

"You're not though," I wrapped my arms around him and nuzzled his neck.

He groaned.

"Come on, let's get this place clean so we can go to bed."

"It's been years since I've been in a bed..." Ryon yawned.

"We were in bed last night."

"Mm. But you kept me awake!"

I rolled my eyes. "You're usually the one who wants to stay up."

"Can't help it," he grinned.

I hated that grin so much that I kissed him to make it disappear.

EIGHTEEN

.---- ---..

To my utter surprise, the next few weeks passed without incident. During the day, I handled most of the house-keeping and preparations for our tavern while Ryon worked in the city. Jaida let him cut his hours in half, giving him a chance to spend time with me...and get much-needed sleep. Each day, the tavern bustled with more life, especially as the winter nights grew long and cold. Coins piled onto our stack, accumulating into a small but comfortable fortune.

Despite our success, our anxiety heightened.

And for good reason.

The more who showed up, the more likely it would be that the Guard would discover us.

Or for Elodie to find out.

Even in the empty house, I often glanced over my shoulder, expecting the Guard to come knocking or Elodie to come screaming. We avoided each other day in and out.

Until one winter morning, when the house snoozed beneath snow flurries.

Elodie approached me for the first time in weeks. Her pregnancy flowering, she rarely slept, her eyes hanging tired and worn. At night, Ryon and I operated our little tavern in silence, praying she would not venture downstairs.

Lucky for us, she often paced on the top floor between the bathroom and her room.

She approached me after Marietta and Ryon left for work, calm and poised. "Nanette?"

I glanced up at her from my cup of tea. "Oh... Elodie."

She fidgeted with her bracelets as she spoke. "I'm heading into the city to go to morning service. I was wondering...would you care to join me? It would mean the world to me...especially as I am going to be moving soon."

I pondered. I had no aspiration to attend a ceremony sanctioned by Elder Vic Tor Cordova and the Order of the Effluvium.

But Elodie stared at me with those longing eyes. It tugged at my heart.

I wanted my sister back.

"Alright. Let me get my coat," I said.

Her smile might have set the field ablaze.

By the time I retrieved my coat, Elodie had already hailed a cabby. As we gathered in the back of the buggy, an awkward silence rocked between us. We hadn't spent time alone like since we last traveled to the Temple together. It was odd. This was the girl I used to explore the swamp beneath Stilette with, laugh and tell stories with, and swoon over lover and romance with, but now we were mere strangers, navigating an unfamiliar and tenuous landscape. I used her own home to harbor criminals. If Elodie caught us, she would be just as much to blame as Ryon, Marietta, and me. Guilt welled in my stomach.

But what about all those people who face persecution for mere tales?

Elodie and Marietta's move to the city couldn't come soon enough.

But today, I had to feign a smile. Pretend everything was okay.

Elodie sliced open the tension a few minutes into our ride. "Are you happy, Nanette?"

I stared at her. "Pardon?"

"You hardly leave home, and you're always mulling about. You look tired too. What has gotten into you?"

"I'm perfectly content!" I argued.

Elodie continued, "Is Mr. Barnes turning you into a housewife? I never took you as one—"

"If you're going to critique Ryon all day, I'll get out of the cab right now!" I glared at her.

"Right, right, I apologize, Dor—Nanette. Marietta wants...I want to mend our relationship if it is alright by you. It would not please Father that we are not getting along, after all. He wanted us to remain together. We're sisters."

"We are," I whispered.

"And even if we disagree on many things, I want to remain sisters."

"As do I. But it might be hard to forget some of what we have said..."

"I do not imagine it will be an easy fix...but there is no reason to continue our spats—"

I wanted to scream. *She* started these spats! But I kept my mouth closed.

Every day, I yearned for my sister back in my life.

Elodie placed her hand on her balloon stomach and continued, "If anything, we can be cordial and civil. After all, I want you to meet my dear babe once she's born."

"Are you sure you're having a girl?"

"It better be. I got everything in pink!"

"A boy can like pink too!"

"Oh, I know that, but I would hate to choose a new name for a boy! I am not naming a boy *Lisa*."

"You don't have a backup name?" I chided.

"*Lester* is what Marietta suggested."

We both giggled. A weight lifted in my chest with the laughter. We hadn't laughed like that in a long time.

I missed it.

But with the laugh, my heart broke a bit as well. I was using her home for my gain...my sister's home!

I couldn't stop now, though.

Father always said that while family is important, stories unite us. How could I live in Rosada without stories? How could I be what Elodie wanted when she tossed tales away?

I had my virtues. I wouldn't abandon them.

The trip into the Capitol proved uneventful. I attended the service with Elodie. Despite my distaste for Elder Vic Tor's words, with his constant preaching to disregard the stories and to give our lives to the Effluvium, Elodie and I didn't argue. Instead, side-by-side as sisters and friends, we ventured into a few shops after the service in search of baby clothes. Elodie even showed me where she and Marietta would live soon.

It was peaceful.

Normal even.

As if, once again, we were friends.

Though the cloud still hung in the air as we returned home.

We went our separate ways back at the house. Elodie joined Marietta upstairs while I sat on the porch, waiting for Ryon to come home from work, as I did most days. I loved running to Ryon and throwing my arms around him, acting like a woman waiting for her husband to come back from war. It might as well be a war, with how tired he was most days. I yearned to take the burden of balancing the two jobs off his shoulders; perhaps someday soon we'd be self-sustaining, and if he desired, he could quit his job in the government.

After all, Ryon was born for these quiet revolutions... not to be a pencil pusher who hardly understood tap-code.

That day he arrived home like all the others. I embraced him on the front lawn. We kissed, our passion yet to be tapered by time, and hurried into the house. Marietta smiled at us as we raced past her and down into our little tavern, clicking the lock shut behind us.

As we had most days, we slowly set up the tables, dancing around each other, stealing kisses and touches as we walked past each other. Some days we ducked behind the counter and let passion grip us for a moment. Not that day, though.

Exhaustion labored its way across Ryon's body. I saw it in the way he walked. He kept his back arched, his hair covering his eyes.

As we put out the last stool, I took his hands. "Go sleep. You need it. I can handle this on my own."

He stroked my cheek. "You sure?"

"Of course. I'm the tavern wench, aren't I?"

"A wench on a bench in the tavern..." He mumbled incomprehensibly.

"Go to bed!" I ushered him to the stairs.

"Okay! Okay. I'll try to stop down again in a few hours, okay?"

"Even if you don't, I can handle it."

He kissed me once before going back up upstairs.

I finished tidying up the tavern. Glasses aligned, drinks set, and a stage glimmered; we were ready for our next batch of storytellers. We averaged well over twenty people a night, each vetted, with passwords handed out with care.

With everything in place, I opened the door to the tunnel. At least ten patrons, half of whom I recognized, waited outside the speakeasy. The password this time was a single phrase.

"Elder Vic Tor is a bastard," the first patron whispered.

And I welcomed them inside my tavern.

The night began without fault. Stories wove their way through the tavern. I manned the bar and monitored the tunnel entrance as more and more people knocked on the door. Few patrons asked where Ryon ran off to, but most of the time, people kept fixated on the stories:

A tale of a woman who climbed a vine up towards the clouds.

A story of a wild beast who builds a city from straw.

A narrative about a doctor who cured the world of all death and disease.

And a plot detailing a magical child who turned the world into cheese.

I leaned against the bar, listening as each story frolicked in the air. Some stories knitted vivid scenes in my imagination. Others, well, they fell flat, receiving a dull round of applause. I still can't get over how storytellers can transform a basic plotline into something unique.

Every hero's story is a little different.

Everyone's life is their own.

I suppose that is the beauty of storytelling. Without it, are we even human?

As I filled up another pitcher of ale, the clattering of pots and pans tugged my attention from a story about a unicorn to the top of the stairs. My stomach dropped.

Another pot chimed.

No one noticed. This wasn't our warning bell.

If it were, everyone would hear.

But someone was in the kitchen.

A light glowed from beneath the door. I held my breath. Perhaps it was just Ryon.

Laughter drowned out another clatter of pans.

The next few moments beat like a drum.

The knob turned.

My heart fell.

It wasn't Ryon.

Before I processed anything, I grabbed the pan hanging on the far wall and banged it in tap-code.

--. ---

Go.

All the patrons stopped.

Then the tavern broke out in chaos.

They moved with the speed and agility of mice. The candles darkened. The stage silenced. And out the patrons left through the tunnels, the last one closing the door in a hushed silence.

But despite the darkness, it was too late.

"WHAT THE FUCK IS GOING ON DOWN HERE?"

It was the first and only time I ever heard Elodie curse.

I lit the gas lantern behind the bar. The room sat empty now, except for Elodie in the stairwell.

We stared at each other among the ransacked tables and chairs, our glares like the broken glass on the floor.

My heart continued in my chest as I met Elodie's piercing glare.

"I can explain." It was a lie. How could I explain... this? We opened an illegal tavern below her house. What else was there to say?

"No." Elodie turned, her fists shaking, her voice quivering, "You have nothing to explain to me. I understand perfectly."

"Elodie—"

But before I said another word, she stormed back upstairs and slammed the door shut.

Leaving me alone.

NINETEEN

.---- ----.

Elodie and Marietta moved out three days later without a word. Even Marietta didn't speak to me, though Ryon informed me it was all part of the façade to keep Elodie content. I couldn't help but wonder at what cost did Marietta lie? If Elodie found out, would it destroy their marriage?

I fell sick after Elodie discovered the tavern. Ryon stayed home, tending to me, letting me sleep in my worries' embrace. In the first day that followed, he got into loud, heated arguments with Elodie in the hallway. It was always the same. She accused him of tainting my mind, of manipulating me with magic, and of taking away my innocence. Whenever Ryon returned, his face bright red with anger, I swore he would burst.

Even after Elodie and Marietta left, the tension remained for a few days. Tears and tremors rocked my sleep. Each night, my dreams recanted Elodie's discovery in shrouds of darkness and fear. Meanwhile, Ryon spent the day pacing, blaming himself for not being down there.

"If I had been there," He kept saying, "I might've noticed the lights. I could have created a distraction or something and then—"

"Stop with the self-pity..." I whispered.

He sank onto the bed, and we wore a shroud of silence through the evening.

Over the course of the week, we settled into this new reticent routine. We crawled out of our own sadness to take in the sudden transformation of the home. It was odd being in the house, though. Every shadow reminded me of Elodie and Marietta.

Although I had avoided Elodie over the past couple of weeks, her constant pattering around the house gave the building life.

Now, everything was dead.

Empty.

But at least it belonged to us.

We came to terms with our new routine. Each morning we woke up and drank tea in the kitchen before Ryon ventured off into the city, and I focused on cleaning the house. Once the building was in tip-top shape, we'd be able to open it up as a bed-and-breakfast. The tavern would run in secret beneath the floorboards, and hopefully, Ryon could quit work to help me.

Yet, during the day, alone with my thoughts, I drifted into that terrible bucket of self-loathing.

I kept myself going for two things: Ryon and the storytellers.

Especially the storytellers.

I wore Brenda Harley's name on my heart. That old woman died for stories. The least we could do, I believed, was give the storytellers a haven to preach.

With Elodie and Marietta gone, we now had more freedom with the tavern. People could cheer, laugh, and sing. Ryon and I also ran the tavern in shifts, giving us both time to rest before the morning. It wouldn't be forever, but we needed the cash.

And damn, did storytellers pay a pretty penny.

I meandered about the house like a shell. I tackled each room, dusting and prepping the beds. I never really ventured to these different rooms, always thinking of them as Elodie's domain. Now that I had the time and freedom, I cleaned each one slowly, leaving Elodie's room for last.

Elodie disinfected the room of anything that resembled her, leaving the walls bare. Well, except for one old law book sitting on her end table.

It still smelled of her disgusting perfume.

"I'm sorry, Elodie," I whispered. Maybe if I had just talked with her about this, things wouldn't have grown hostile.

But I was doing what I knew was right.

Stories needed room to breathe.

I flipped through the pages. A bookmark rested on Statute 19-10-20-B: *Storytelling by the general populace is outlawed on the counts of hearsay, rumors, malice, and destruction.*

Below the statute, a statement by the Prime Senator who pushed for the new law followed:

58th day of summer, Rosadian Year 812 — It is on this day, we decree, that storytelling is no longer permitted. We have collected all fictions and burned them, but for a few harmless tales for children and our sanctioned history.

This extremity was necessary in protecting Rosada. After we abolished magic in 749, we thought the terrors against Rosada had long but ended. We did not expect stories to inspire our adolescents to rise against our government, to seek magic, or tarnish the name of our sanctuary, the Order of the Effluvium.

There were many senators against this notion, but they offered us no other choice. Fiction, stories, rumors—they only divide this great nation. They distract us from the guiding hand of the Effluvium. Without stories, Rosada could become a utopia as our dear founders intended.

Now, our people can see the Effluvium with a clear mind.

As we decree.

I stormed from the room, collapsing into a chair in the kitchen, still clutching the book. My fingers tore through the pages, each statute and article piercing my heart. So much for feeling sympathetic about Elodie! She must have left this here. I knew it!

I kept flipping through the pages as I waited for Ryon to get home. Self-pity and anger continued tapping into my psyche. Wouldn't I yell at Ryon for behaving like this? Of course I would! This was ridiculous!

I understood the risks of starting this tavern. I expected she would disapprove.

This was my choice.

So why should I care she was trying to scare me?

Ryon returned as I threw the book across the room. He jumped as it hit the floor, his eyes wide.

He picked up the book and glanced it over once. "Rosadian Law?"

"Elodie left it. Bookmarked a page about that story-telling statute initiated fifty years ago. Must have been to scare me."

"Don't let it get to you. She's being stubborn as a mule."

"It's not getting to me! I'm fine!" The furor in my voice trembled.

"Nan—"

"Really, I'm fine."

He took my fingers and stroked them gently. "If you don't want to continue this, let me know. We can stop. We can be normal...people..." His voice hung on those last words.

I met his gaze. "No. I want to do this."

It wasn't a lie.

He shuffled his feet.

I continued, "I'm struggling, that's all. This has been a wild year. Just last year, I was living with my father and never imagined coming to the Capitol or meeting the love of my life." I took his hands. "It's been a lot. But I wouldn't trade it for the world."

Ryon's eyes lit up as I kissed his hand.

Things would be okay.

Over the following weeks, we settled into a routine. Patrons filled the upstairs lodging, and downstairs, the storytellers bustled and laughed. We began harboring a steady stream of income, and Ryon reduced his time working for Jaida to one day a week.

His change in workload didn't come with a wave of happiness, though.

After bathing one early morning, I strolled downstairs to meet with Ryon, bypassing a few guests in the hall. I waved to them, then entered the parlor. Ryon had yet to leave for work, his nose buried in the Capitol's gazette.

"Good morning." I leaned forward to kiss his forehead.

He didn't say a word.

"Ryon? Are you okay?" I sat down next to him.

He pointed at the newspaper headline. My jaw dropped as I read it.

Utopian Project Approved Across the Province

In a stunning victory, the Senate Rosada approved of the Utopian Project. Captain Steven Cordova will lead the project with the help of Senator Dally from Knoll's Gully.

I couldn't read anymore. Tears budded in my eyes.

"Even after everything, Calvin couldn't convince enough people," Ryon muttered. "Jaida was antsy the other day. This is why, I guess."

"They're going to build more pits," I said, astonished.

"Yes."

I shook my head. "We're needed now more than ever."

"I think that's why Jaida told me I could start reducing my hours. This"—he glanced towards the kitchen— "is more important."

"Are you going in today?" I asked.

"No. Not today."

"Good."

We finished our tea and biscuits, waiting as the last patrons left our inn from the conglomerate of rooms. Then, we dressed to leave, preparing to venture into the capital like we did in our early romance. Had we really met only six months earlier? It felt like a lifetime!

We had a usual routine when we arrived at the plaza. We posted up flyers for our traditional inn while speaking in secret to storytellers to offer the passcode. Often, Ryon babbled about the architecture, informing me of the history and stories behind each. It was just like those days we spent, talking in the middle of the night, enthralled with one another.

Today was different, though. Ryon didn't have the usual bounce. The repercussions of the vote hung stiffly in the air.

More Pits would decorate the landscape.

They would take more storytellers away.

And there was little we could do to stop it.

At the edge of the plaza, as we rested on the bench hand-in-hand, our somber mood broke. At least for a moment.

Because there, in the plaza that day, I saw *them* again.

When I saw them crossing the road, approaching me, my heart leapt into my throat. Like a portrait of two glistening deities, they shimmered.

Their eyes locked with mine.

"Gisela? Yeshua? Is that you?" I cried out.

"Nanette! Darling!" Gisela skipped to me, dragging Yeshua by his wrist. "It has been too long!"

I embraced her and Yeshua, then turned back to Ryon. "Oh! This is my fiancé! Ryon, this is Gisela and Yeshua."

"Ah yeah, I've heard much about both of you." Ryon beamed at them, his cheeks turning pink.

I nudged him.

"It's a pleasure." Yeshua grinned, his voice soft as a pillow. "I'm glad Nanette has made a way for herself."

"It's been quite an adventure." I smiled at Ryon, then back at Yeshua and Gisela. "What have you two been up to!?! I thought you were heading back to Heims! I didn't think I'd see you again!"

"We were, we were," Gisela acknowledged. "But it is so brutal during the winter. We got to Waltersberg in Kainan and decided it was best to turn around. We looped around Knoll and started back towards the Capitol. Unfortunately, a few members of our caravan got sick, so we might just be here for a while."

"Oh, I'm sorry. Do you need anything from us?" I asked.

"We have already made accommodations for our sick. The rest of us are staying at our campsite. Thank you for offering, though." Gisela squeezed my hand. Her skin was as smooth as I remembered.

"If you need anything, though, we run an inn on the far side of town," Ryon replied.

Some people would have been uncomfortable with Gisela and Yeshua. Not Ryon, though. I was open about what happened while I journeyed with the caravan. Ryon accepted it, like any other story. I never wanted to go back to that life; while Gisela and Yeshua had their own beauty, I had Ryon. That was all I wanted.

Even as I stared at Yeshua and Gisela, they no longer bore that same aura of fascination and allure. They were just two people.

Ryon was the one who made my heart flutter.

Gisela smiled at Ryon and me. "We may just take you up on that offer one night. A fresh set of linens would be most enjoyable."

"I would love it if you stopped by. We must catch up," I plead with the two of them.

They nodded. "We shall see."

Three days later, Yeshua and Gisela stopped by our inn with a new flame on their heels. He was a skinny fellow, with round glasses, slick blond hair, and a straight nose, and inexperienced in romancing, by my guess.

There was nothing remarkable about him otherwise. He may have been any other man in the city.

They vanished in what used to be Elodie's room until the early evening. Ryon and I had gathered downstairs, preparing for the influx of storytellers, when finally, both Gisela and Yeshua emerged from their chambers. Their associate, for lack of a better word, was nowhere to be seen.

"Where's your friend?" I smirked.

"Oh, Ralph? He's asleep," Gisela yawned. "We tired the poor fellow out."

"What are you two up to?" Yeshua's attention drifted to the door to the cellar. His brow furrowed.

"Oh, um," I glanced at Ryon. I trusted Yeshua and Gisela, of course. They weren't from Rosada. I doubt they cared about the illegality of storytelling. Yet I didn't want to betray Ryon and give away our secret. We set this up with a reason.

Ryon saved me. "We have an operation going on downstairs."

"That implies you're doing something illegal." Yeshua raised both his eyebrows.

"Maybe a little..." I flushed.

"Are you going to tell us, or are we going to have to find out?" Gisela pried; her ruby-painted lips pulled in a wide smile.

I glanced again at Ryon. He nodded.

"Come on. We'll show you." I opened the door as I spoke, leading them down into our hidden tavern.

As I expected, Yeshua's and Gisela's jaws dropped over what we put together. They admired the structure with awe, commenting on the layout and the intricate plan with the tunnels.

"I have not seen something like this in a long time!" Gisela applauded, running her hand over the tunnel door. A few storytellers pushed past them, muttering the password "There's a cat on my head" to Ryon as they shoved past him. In the short time since we opened that evening, we already had twenty people in the small tavern, almost at our full capacity!

"It's amazing someone has not caught you yet," Yeshua said.

Gisela rolled her eyes. "Do not mind him. You know how we worry."

"We have a system in place." I took Gisela's hand. "I'm not the same foolish girl you met all those months ago."

"No, you have blossomed. And found yourself a wonderful man as well. I am envious of him."

"You have Yeshua... and the boy upstairs... and others..." I flushed.

"But I remember all who I love equally. I'll never forget our time together. Neither will Yeshua."

I hugged Gisela tight. I didn't realize how much I missed her and Yeshua. They helped me escape myself in a time of sorrow. Would I have been as adventurous without them? Would I have pursued Ryon's hand?

Once Gisela released me, I turned towards Ryon. His eyes sparkled as they caught mine.

"I love you." I mouthed in his direction.

He grinned.

Hand-in-hand, we sat on the counter, listening as a storyteller wove a story about dragons and shadows. Yeshua removed his oud and strummed along with it while Gisela hopped onto the piano to play an equally provocative tune. It spun around the room, and with it, Ryon and I danced.

Perhaps everything would work out in the end. We had this under control.

Now, we just had to live.

TWENTY

.●--- -----

Throughout the next month, Yeshua and Gisela often visited with their enchanted lover, sleeping in Elodie's old room, before joining us in the tavern late at night. The young fellow, Ralph, sometimes joined them, enamored with the stories, his eyes wide with wonder. It made his nose look smaller whenever he gaped.

Ryon and I benefited monetarily, but that meant nothing to me. Sure, it kept the roof over our heads and let us upgrade the tavern, but I relished in the smiles the tavern brought. So many stories waltzed through the air.

Ryon developed a new pep in his step with each passing day. He even started talking about buying a horse and buggy for when we wanted to go into the city or visit his parents. Sometimes, he even mentioned buying his parents a new home.

A dream. But I didn't dare taint his excitement.

We never abandoned our vigilance. Constantly, we worried that the guard watched over our shoulder or that a spy would sneak in and shut down the tavern.

I guess those fears weren't unfounded. Each day, guards wrangled storytellers in the streets, and our storytellers spoke with fear in their eyes. It echoed through the tavern. Patrons spoke of running away with the caravan once it departed, although according to Gisela and Yeshua, that was still weeks away. Snow and storms struck down the landscape, encasing the land in white; travel by foot would cause certain death.

The steam engine trains provided little comfort as they trudged along the landscape, leading guards to and from the Capitol to enact the Utopia Project across the province.

Our tavern provided at least a bit of comfort while dark winter fell upon us all.

We played a waiting game.

And in it, our tavern grew.

As did our love.

Ryon and I never stopped smiling, never stopped laughing. I loved him with every fraction of my body. Elodie once warned me the spark would die, but we never had a spark. No. Our love was a bonfire. We built it out of sticks and logs, kindling it with every word and kiss. Some days it burned us. Other days, it gave us light.

Because isn't that love, in the end? You don't want to grab a spark because sparks fade.

Fire gives light.

Everything was going our way.

But in the back of my mind, I knew things would change. It was only a matter of time.

Marietta brought change with a knock on the door and a tired smile on her lips. With it, she carried wonderful news: Elodie had given birth to a bouncing baby boy named Lester. I couldn't restrain my laughter. Elodie was so certain she would have a girl. But she gave birth to a son! Not a daughter! Lester! Not Lisa!

While she didn't join my laughter, Marietta smiled, walking around the house she used to call home to admire our changes, before taking a seat at the table beside Ryon. She ran her fingers along the banister. "I am sad I cannot raise little Lester in this house. But it's for the best. Elodie is much happier in the city."

"I am sure she is happy that Lester isn't kicking her ribs anymore either," I simpered.

"That too," Marietta chuckled, then her face grew heavy. "You should come visit."

"I doubt Elodie wants to see me."

"Yes, but *I* want to see you. Both of you." She glanced at Ryon.

"You're seeing us now," Ryon replied.

"No, I mean, I want you to meet Lester. He deserves to know his aunt and uncle." She smiled sadly. There was pain in her face I hadn't seen before, her dark eyes heavy.

"Is everything okay, Marietta?" I asked.

"Yes. As expected, we're tired. Newborns never sleep," Marietta half-laughed, then met my gaze. "I really think Elodie needs you, Nanette. She needs her sister."

"She doesn't, though."

"I think that's a lie. And I think you need her too." Marietta squeezed my hand. "Please come by this week. Both of you. I want us to be a family again."

"Yes, but..."

"Please," Marietta begged. "Just for a half hour. Meet Lester. Be with Elodie. I think she misses you, even she won't admit it."

After one last glance with Ryon, I agreed. I knew Marietta meant it. Besides, I wanted to see my nephew.

I just hoped Elodie would be as welcoming as Marietta claimed.

A few days later, Ryon and I ventured to the Capitol. We went our separate ways in the plaza, with Ryon going to give a password to the storytellers while I visited Elodie. It was better that way, we decided.

I doubted Elodie wanted anything to do with Ryon, anyway.

Marietta waited outside their small apartment overlooking the plaza. She smiled at me, her lips painted magenta, her cosmetics smudged as if she never had the chance to remove it from days prior. A babe screamed just beyond the threshold.

"Long night?" I asked. I expected it would be. That's what kids do.

It was right then, asking Marietta about her own child, I wondered if I would ever yearn for motherhood. Ryon never mentioned wanting children. It never even crossed my mind. I only cared about the tavern.

While part of me wanted a child someday, there was so much else I wanted to do in this world. The constant questions lingered in my mind: how could I raise children if stories had to be told in the shadows? How could I tell them not to play with their imaginary friends? Or tell them to only listen to facts?

This wasn't the world in which I wanted to bring kids, and while I didn't think I could change it, the least I could do was make it safer with a silly storytelling speakeasy.

I took a deep breath before I entered the apartment.

The apartment matched Elodie in every aspect. Decorated with the latest wares, color-coordinated to the point of precision, I expected nothing different. A shelf of books bordered the far wall, where Elodie sat in the chair, nursing baby Lester, her head hanging from exhaustion. Their parlor was an almost exact copy of the one back in the tavern, with bookshelves lining the walls and that hunting rifle hanging on the wall. My heart broke at the sight. I wanted to hold her and offer help. But she didn't meet my gaze. She didn't even acknowledge me.

Her attention was solely on the child, who continued to fidget and wail.

Marietta approached her, "Elodie, your sister is here to visit."

I held my breath. She didn't budge.

"She wants to meet Lester," Marietta continued.

No response.

"Elodie—" I stepped forward.

"Go away," she hissed.

"I—"

"You betrayed my trust."

"Elodie, I..." My shoulders fell. "You're right. I did. But it was of my own accord. I knew exactly what I was doing. But..." I approached her. "If you had seen what I saw when I ended up in that explosion...and the way it affected people...you might react the same."

"You speak like I am blind." Elodie scoffed. "I've seen what you've seen. Why do you think I left the Academy?"

"You said you got caught up in the life of the Capitol."

"Yes, but only because I realized advocates here did not stand for righteousness. They stand for the law. They're puppets. Fools. So, I moved on from my heroic fantasies. It'd be wise if you do the same."

"Don't you want a better future for your son?"

Elodie glanced back down at Lester.

I continued, "It's not going to get better if we sit and wait."

Elodie shook her head. Without a word, she handed Lester to Marietta and left the room. The silence followed after her, stalking like a mere shadow on the wall, but for a hum of commotion outside the building.

I sighed, fidgeting with the edge of my dress. What could I say? The rift had grown too deep between us.

I had to move on; I had a tavern to run, storytellers to protect, and a life to live.

Trying my best to shed my sadness, I let Marietta put Lester in my arms. The child wailed as soon as I brought him close to rock him. Marietta adjusted my arms twice, but despite all our best efforts, he continued to shriek. I tried to smile and coo at him, but it was as if some puppeteer controlled my actions. All the while, my ears popped with my aching heart.

After a few more minutes of Lester's agitation, Marietta brought the child into his bedroom then led me back downstairs. She kept pausing to say something, then shook her head. There had been an essence of hope in the air when I arrived; she wanted Elodie and I to move past our difference.

Yet this wound was too fresh and deep. A single apology could not heal our relationship.

Perhaps in due time, things might change.

As we walked downstairs, shouts and screams bustled from the street up into the walkway. I glanced at Marietta, then raced down the path into the plaza.

There, in the plaza outside Elodie and Marietta's apartment, chaos ensued, coupled with screams and cursing. People ran towards the Temple for salvation, while others ducked into the shops and beneath benches. Captain Cordova's guards piled into the streets, marching with their usual sleazy swagger. Each of his subordinates moved identically to the next, no life in their face or their voice. They were in a choir, singing songs with gunshots pummeling through the air. Smoke captured the edges of buildings.

"What's happening?!" I shouted over the commotion.

No one stopped to answer.

Guards dragged individuals out of alleyways, tugging away their instruments, breaking their possessions, and throwing books into a fire outside the Gallery. I recognized a few of the storytellers from my tavern. Their cries rose with the destruction.

As did the guards' cackles.

"Nanette!" Marietta raced to my side.

"What happened? Everything was quiet!" I shouted.

"Nanette—"

"I have to help—"

"NANETTE!" Marietta turned me around to face a nearby alleyway, where a group of guards dragged a horde of storytellers and performers into the plaza.

My attention fell only on one.

"RYON!"

TWENTY-ONE

..--- .----

"NO! RYON!"

I continued screaming Ryon's name as Marietta dragged me back into the building. She forced me down onto the steps, ordering me to breathe, inhaling on one and exhaling on two. My head spun, and my heart raced. All I thought about was Ryon. Blood dripped from his face, his hair damp with sweat, and his body was limp with defeat. His eyes hung with emptiness, lacking their excitement and luster. I had to get to him.

He was only guilty of inviting people to our tavern. Nothing more.

And I repeated that sentiment repeatedly to Marietta.

He did nothing wrong.

"Nanette. Nanette. Calm down. Hysterics will do you no good." Marietta gripped my shoulders.

I fell into her embrace, sobbing. I needed the hug more than I cared to admit. Part of me wished Elodie would appear in the stairwell and comfort me as well, just like she did when Mama died. But it was just Marietta and me, alone, as the commotion dwindled to a half-sung tune. My heart thudded and raced.

This was all a mistake.

Maybe Elodie was right.

Ryon and I should have behaved ourselves.

But the guard would still arrest storytellers, even if we kept our heads bowed.

The cycle would continue.

"I need to find him—they're taking him to the Pit! I have to get there and break him out or something!" A wheeze escaped my lips. "I need to see him."

"Nanette, breathe. Do not be rash." Marietta said. "You have connections. Could your friend in the Capitol help?"

"Jaida..." I mumbled. "Yes, you're right. I should...I should go talk with her right now!" I leapt to my feet.

"Nanette! Sit! You need a chance to calm down!"

"I can't wait. The longer I wait...please, Marietta, I need to go see Jaida."

Marietta sighed. "Are you sure you're okay to go?"

Tears continued to sting the corners of my eyes, but I nodded, gulping down another tenuous sob. The sooner I acted, the sooner Ryon would be home.

Or so I hoped.

With another embrace, I said goodbye to Marietta and walked back into the plaza. The commotion ceased as fast as it began. A few vendors and patrons in the streets reemerged from behind benches and from the shop doors while the few remaining guards resumed their positions against the walls. It was as if a raid had never happened. The only sign of struggle came from the smoke lacing through the air like spiderwebs and the distant rumble of horses and buggies rushing away from the city.

I eyed a couple of the guards as I walked towards the Capitol Building. They all looked the same, with their slicked-back hair and stone-cold eyes. Who took Ryon? Did they take him to the Pit? Or worse? Had they already beaten the truth out of him? Was it okay for me to go home? Or would guards be waiting for me there?

No. Ryon was stronger than that. He wouldn't falter.

But what about the other storytellers?

No. I had to believe in them. All of them. Humans exist to tell stories. Take that away, and we're only the demons the Order claims exist.

By the time I reached the Capitol Building, I had reconnected with my confidence, casting aside the last bout of tears and carrying my head high. It was a weird feeling, entering those double doors again. They were heavier than I remembered, and as I strode in, I swore all eyes focused on me.

I rewrote history.

I wrote the truth.

But they didn't know that. To them, I was the one who caused Captain Oberland to lose his job. The long-respected captain had fallen because of me.

But did that matter if he caused others harm? Did his friendly façade mean anything if others cried because of his deeds?

I didn't speak to anyone as I marched through the halls, up to the second floor where Jaida's office waited. The door hung ajar.

"Jaida?" I nudged the door open. "Hello? Jaida?"

Her office sat empty. Completely empty. Not a trinket in sight.

"Oh no... not you too..."

I collapsed on the floor, burying my face in my hands. *No.*

I lost my sister, my fiancé, and now my friend. Hadn't we planned a quiet trip into the city? We expected terror in other waves, down in the tavern or in aisles of story-tellers.

Not today.

I lost track of long I sat on the floor crying. In repetitive circles, I kept telling myself to stand up already; this wouldn't help! Misery was unbecoming of me. But the stress and fear overwhelmed me. I might never have moved... if a kind voice didn't pull me from my despair. "Miss Ivans?"

I turned. Senator Heartz stood in the doorway, exhaustion prickling the corners of his face.

I wiped the snot from my nose. "Sorry, Senator. I did not mean to intrude."

"It is a'ight, Miss Ivans. What are you doing here?"

"Oh...I was coming to see Jaida..."

"Jaida didn't have time to tell you?"

I shook my head.

"She left yesterday to head back to Newbird's Arm for the time being. She's trying to stop the construction of the Pit." Senator Heartz's face fell. "Did she tell you that the notion passed? Pits are to be established across the country. I tried my best to stop it, but...it wasn't enough. There are too many adversaries in the Senate."

"Yes, we saw in the paper. But we didn't have a chance to speak with her."

"It happened quickly if I say so myself. But her leaving is a necessity. I don't have the time to spare. But she plans to come back once we have a senatorial recess. She only emptied her office for safety, not fear. Guards are always snooping around, after all." Senator Heartz placed a strong hand on my shoulder. "But I fear your mood is not just for my sister, is that correct?"

"That's correct," I whispered. "They...the Guard...they arrested Ryon. I...I need to see him. Can you help?"

"I would love to help, Miss Ivans. But I believe you already know where they are taking Ryon."

I stared at the senator, then towards the windows. Yes, of course, I knew.

It didn't mean I wouldn't try to stop it.

Without questioning the circumstances of Ryon's arrest, Senator Heartz hailed a cabby to take us to the Pit on the outside of town. He heard the general idea of what happened in the square, and as we rode to find Ryon, he caught me up on the details.

"Cordova got whiff of a new network of storytellers," Senator Heartz whispered to me. "Jaida and I thought it was your tavern and planned to warn you, but he acted faster. Rounded up the storytellers he could find in the alleys. Recognized most of them, I guess. Figured that would stop it."

"And Ryon got caught up in the mess..." I replied.

"As it seems."

I hung my head, not willing to speak as the cabby bumped along the road. Did it always take this long to get to the village on the outskirts of the Capitol? With Ryon, it never felt like any time at all! But every passing second meant the longer it would take for Ryon to be free.

I didn't dare lift my head as we passed by his parents' farm. For years, he'd grown up with the Pit glowering at him. Now he was its prisoner. Ryon always understood the risks of his rebellion, but part of me felt like this was my fault! Why did we have to go visit Elodie and Marietta today? Why couldn't we go tomorrow? Or next week?

Or never?

We arrived in the heart of the village, a short walk away from the Pit. Before Senator Heartz could stop me, I raced to the fence, my heart pounding, dirt kicking up over my shoes. I peered through a hole in the fence at the sight. Ever since Ryon first showed me the Pit, I hadn't dared to take another look. It was just as terrifying as I remembered: children laying in squalor, adults charred and worn, and the elderly withering away half dead. My heart ached. I couldn't imagine Ryon, my bright and talkative Ryon, becoming so worn.

"Miss Ivans," Senator Heartz joined my side, "Come with me."

I glanced through the fence one last time, then followed the senator. We strode in silence for a few minutes until rounding the corner where the Guards stood positioned on the road leading into the Pit.

A large metal gate stood between two watchtowers, while Guards with their usual glares waited undeterred.

"Stay close to me," Senator Heartz whispered.

I stood by his side as we approached. A guard repositioned his pistol.

"Who goes there?" The Guard barked.

"Good afternoon, Lieutenant. I'm Senator Heartz from the Newbird Region." The senator removed a badge from his coat. "I'm here on official senate duties. They would like me to take stock of those you arrested from the raids today."

"No one informed me of this." The guard replied.

"Does the Senate have to give notice to every lieutenant in the Capitol?"

The Guard squirmed in frustration. "We have a procedure, sir."

"Yes, and this raid today avoided half of them."

I admired the senator's guile. His courage to stand before the Guard with a firm heart placed a new sapling of determination in my soul.

I will find Ryon.

The Guard looked the senator up and down, then glanced at me. "And who is this?"

"This is my scribe. She will be taking notes for me," The senator said.

"She doesn't look like a scribe. Those are commoner clothes."

"I had off today." I formulated my lie in haste. "I was stopping by the Capitol to retrieve something from my desk when Senator Heartz asked I join him."

"Hmph." I couldn't tell if the Guard believed us or not, but he didn't really have much of a choice. He grunted to himself, then unlocked the gate a smidge so we could enter.

The gates screeched, sending the hairs on my neck standing on edge.

The entrance of the Pit reminded me of stories about war. Wagons and tents lay positioned at the front, with Guards gathered in groups. They acted human there: huddled together in conversation, smoking, and playing card games. Just beyond where they ate and drank, vagrants sat in squalor.

I scanned the campsite in horror, trying to find Ryon among it all. A few trucks sat parked against the far corner of the site, with rows of individuals chained to the wall. My heart leapt as I saw a dollop of flaming red hair sitting with them.

Senator Heartz motioned me along with him. "Follow my lead, a'ight? I'll distract the Guard, so you may speak with him."

We strode over with purpose, but my stomach remained in knots. Was this my future? The Pit wreaked of garbage and feces, death loitering on the arms of smoke in the air.

A captain marched before the prisoners, a club in hand. He hit a few over the head as they squirmed and protested.

Even Ryon.

"Excuse me? Captain?" Senator Heartz strode over to the captain. He gave me a quick nod, and as the guard turned his back on the prisoners, I raced over to Ryon.

He raised his head as I approached. Blood dripped from a cut on his forehead. His voice scratched the air. "Nan?"

"Ryon!" I restrained the urge to hug him, to touch him, to kiss him, instead keeping myself a couple of steps back.

"What're you doing here? You'll get caught—"

"Senator Heartz." I moved my head towards the senator.

"Still...you...Nan...I..." For once, Ryon was at a loss for words. He lowered his head, staring at his bruised hands. "I was talking too much. I'm sorry."

"It's not your fault." I choked on my tears.

"No, I...when I was giving out flyers, these kids, they asked if I knew any stories. So, I started telling a pretty pitiful one, and other storytellers joined in to save me from humiliation. A guard caught notice, and I...I should have seen him. He was right there!"

"No, Ryon, no," I said. "Senator Heartz says Captain Cordova planned this raid. It wasn't because of you."

"They overheard—"

"The raid was happening no matter what. Please, don't blame yourself. We'll...I'll get you out of here. Whatever the bail is, whatever I need to do...I'll buy your freedom!"

"Nanette..."

"I can sell the tavern or...or get another job! I will not let you stay here!"

"Nan—"

"I'm sure the tavern could fetch a pretty penny—"

"Nanette!" He stopped me. "Don't sell the tavern!"

"But...nothing good comes of it," I choked. "I can't run it alone."

"Yes, but it's your baby. You have put so much work into it." Ryon flinched. Blood started pooling from his wound again. "Think on it. Promise me you won't sell. Just keep working, saving, and...and hopefully, I can get out of here. Then we can figure it out from there."

"But what if they want to take you away? Or if you get sick? I can't let you end up like the others here."

"Then we'll regroup. But keep fighting, Nanette. That's who you are. You're a fighter. It's why I love you."

The floodgates threatened to reopen, but I held back my tears again. "I won't rest until I get you out."

"I don't doubt you."

I gazed at him a few moments longer, yearning to touch his face and wipe the blood from his cheeks.

My heart sank deeper in my stomach as I watched him fidget. The realization came as a question. "What about your medication? The sugar medication?"

"I'm sure I'll be okay," Ryon whispered.

"You need it, though."

"Ahem, Miss Ivans?" Senator Heartz called. "Do you have the count complete? We don't want to overstay our welcome here. The Guard is quite busy."

"Oh, uh, yes, sir!" I called back, keeping a certain essence of poise. "Coming!"

I glanced back at Ryon one last time and murmured, "Take care of yourself the best you can. I love you."

"Go be as stunning as a sunset, Nanette," Ryon whispered back.

I held his gaze until he became nothing more than a faceless prisoner. Then I returned to Senator Heartz's side, trying my best not to draw attention from the Guard while my heart crumbled into a thousand pieces.

TWENTY-TWO

..- -- ..- --

A week passed. I visited Ryon twice in the Pit. We sat at the edge of the fence, our fingers touching through the small holes that were big enough to slip through a few vials of the sugar medicine as well as some needles. He pocketed them quickly before the guards noticed. Yet neither of us was certain how long it would last. Ryon looked worse each day, though, the bruises on his face turning a malicious yellow while he limped through the Pit with lost swagger. He had dropped weight in haste, and his usually vibrant red hair was more like a dull flame.

How long could he survive such an ordeal?

I didn't tell his parents he was there, keeping my face covered as I ventured through the village to the Pit's wall. It was for the best; Ryon even asked me not to tell them. It would break his mother's heart, worry his sisters, and anger his father.

"Let's try to avoid any more family quarrels," Ryon chuckled as he brushed the tips of my fingers.

I couldn't bring myself to respond, bowing my head and choking back further tears.

The cost to buy his freedom was insurmountable, though. When I discovered the hefty fine, I thought I would faint. The only way I could afford that involved selling the tavern.

But Ryon was right, as per usual.

I couldn't give up on the tavern. We anticipated the risks. The fight would continue.

How else would anyone learn about this if not for stories?

Instead, I put every penny into savings, spending only on the essentials and eating nothing more than rice, bread, and potatoes.

After a week of keeping the tavern running with few storytellers, I garnered a tenth of what I would need to bail Ryon out.

That meant Ryon needed to stay in the Pit for ten weeks. I doubted I had that long. The Guard might move him. Or he might get sick.

My mind raced day and night, trying to think of some way I could help Ryon. But it all came up blank.

Marietta visited me a couple times. She worried I would do something rash. But I reveled in the silence instead. I needed that silence to figure out what to do. These constant visitors proved as only a distraction!

I floated countless ideas: breaking Ryon out and running to Volfium, setting the fence aflame, leading a coup against the government. But all of it seemed ridiculous.

Really, the best option was to pay for Ryon's freedom.

By the end of the week, my goal was simple: to refashion life in the tavern, bring new storytellers, and let our voices scream. I took up Ryon's duty, whispering the newest passwords to familiar storytellers, sometimes even delivering it in tap-code, before returning home to start another round of drinks for the night.

Sleep became the enemy. I even gave up my bedroom so more people could spend the night. When I slept, it was in winks, either at the kitchen table, down in the tavern, or on the sofa. A part of me realized how ridiculous this seemed. All of this for one person?

But I loved him. Didn't that matter? He'd fought to be better than his family, to find independence. He got there. The least I could do was help him live that destiny.

Selfishly, I wanted him back as well. He was my fiancé.

He was my first love.

And my only love.

So I kept working. I wrote to Jaida, telling her of my conundrum. But otherwise, I was alone.

At least until Yeshua and Gisela came knocking on my front door again.

Ryon remained imprisoned for a week and a half when they came. I was busy sweeping the kitchen, operating on three hours of sleep, when the knock rocked the room. I jumped, spewing out a stream of curse words.

"Nanette! It is Gisela and Yeshua!"

I dropped the broom and rushed over, apologizing profusely. As the door swung open, I almost threw myself at the two of them, relieved to see another bout of familiar faces.

I stopped myself. Their squirrely friend with wide glasses stood behind them, his thin eyebrows raised.

"Oh, hello." I bowed.

"You remember Ralph, yes?" Yeshua asked.

"Yes, of course. Hello, Ralph."

Their friend lowered his head.

"I didn't know you were still in town," I said to Gisela and Yeshua, disappointment clear in my tone. Why hadn't they stopped by sooner? Why did they leave me to navigate this alone?

Gisela answered with a squeeze of my hands. "After the storyteller raids, we stayed on the outskirts of town for a bit. But we worried about you, dear."

That mere act of affection filled my throat with tears. I lowered myself to the ground and wallowed with the events about Ryon pooling out of my lips. Gisela held me tight, letting me sob, while Yeshua stroked back my hair. Ralph stood behind them like an awkward puppy. I needed Gisela and Yeshua more than anything right now. Not for romance. I needed their love, their care, like the way a sibling might love their sister.

I needed support.

Gisela handed me a kerchief. I dabbed my eyes, feeling a weight tumbling from my shoulders.

That's when my gaze met Ralph, looking over the rims of his round glasses.

"Sorry. I didn't mean to spill that all at once. I just..." I glanced at my fingers.

"Sounds like you need a packed house," Ralph stated with a shrug.

"I can't do that without risking my safety."

Gisela patted Ralph on the back, then beamed at me. "Leave that to us, Nanette. We have connections."

"I..."

Yeshua rubbed my fingers again. "Trust us. You'll be able to get Ryon out within a week. We have friends in many places."

"But what if someone—"

"Trust us, Nanette. We're just as much at risk as you are." Gisela winked. "We like a good story too."

While I trusted Yeshua and Gisela with my life, I still readied the tavern with additional safety measures. I rigged up thin strings outside to ring the alarm bells and hung more pots and pans on the walls to use as alerts. What good would it be if the guard arrested me?

If I knew anything about Yeshua and Gisela, I knew they were relentless and wouldn't take no for an answer.

And that night, when they came with over fifty individuals in organized droves, providing me three times my daily profits, I almost kissed them out of sheer joy! Patrons packed the tavern to the brim, and at this rate, I could get Ryon out in two weeks!

Over those next couple of days, I operated in a cloud of euphoria. I sent a message to Marietta about my good fortune. I even wrote to Jaida and her brother, informing them soon Ryon would be home free.

Part of me ached to do more. I wanted to help everyone in the Pit. But I was no heroine. Not like that.

There would be others, with grander stories than mine, who would put an end to this Utopian Project. But those are stories for another time.

For five nights, everything ran perfectly. The tavern averaged at least fifty people at night, with every room filled until the next morning. I fell asleep in the chair by the entrance after the tavern went silent, where people left me coins on my lap as they exited in silence. In the morning, I woke up with gold pieces aplenty.

The afternoon following the sixth evening of success, I received another surprise visitor.

I sat in the parlor eating with Gisela, Yeshua, and Ralph, running through numbers when the doorbell rang. I hopped to my feet, taken aback as the door opened.

Elodie stood on the other side.

I gawked. "El-Elodie!"

"Hello, Nanette." Elodie's eyes hung.

"What brings you here?" I asked.

"Oh...I was out and about..." She peered into the foyer. "The house looks like it is doing well."

"It is doing fantastic. Do you...do you want to come in?"

Elodie shook her head. "No. I am here to extend an invitation."

"An invitation?"

"For dinner. Tonight." Elodie tucked her hair behind her ear as she spoke. "You can close the tavern for one night, right? Come eat dinner with us, spend the night with Marietta and Lester. We would really appreciate it."

My heart sank. I wanted more than anything to say yes.

But time was short.

"Elodie, can we do it next week? I would absolutely love to, but with Ryon imprisoned, I cannot abandon this. I am only a few days short of bailing him out of there."

"It is really important you come tonight." Elodie held her ground, still not meeting my gaze.

"Why tonight?"

Elodie snapped, "Does it matter why? I'm trying to mend our relationship, Nanette! Don't you want to fix this? Daddy would want us to be friends again."

"I know..." I took her hands, trying my best to avoid this fight, "But I don't know if they'll keep Ryon here or ship him off. This is my only chance. You would do the same for Marietta."

Elodie pulled away. "But I would do more to protect my sister!"

"What are you talking about?"

Elodie's shoulders relaxed. "I'm worried, that's all. Your tavern is... I'm worried more people know about it than you want."

"It wouldn't surprise me."

"No! Dor—Nanette! Marietta was helping with some expense reports. They're focusing more and more on shutting down these sorts of operations. Then I was in the Temple, and I overhead Elder Vic Tor and his brother talking. They are going to be checking the outskirts of the city! Perhaps you should stop for a bit...at least the storytelling side of things. Until they pass."

"That's where I make most of my money. No one would come here otherwise!"

"Nan—"

Gisela called from the other room, "Nanette? Who is it? What's wrong?"

"I'll be right there!" I shouted back.

Gisela entered the foyer, a smile tugging at her lips. "Oh! You must be Elodie! You're exactly as Nanette described!"

Elodie glared at Gisela, then back at me. "Please. Just consider what I said. I want what is in your best interest."

"I'll...try."

"Then try harder." Elodie turned, rejoining her cabby on the road.

Once Elodie reached the road, Gisela inquired, "What was that about?"

"She thinks the tavern is in danger..." I scowled.

"Nonsense!" Gisela shook her head in disbelief. "We have vetted everyone—"

"Yes, but maybe we should tone it down for the next couple of nights. Fewer people, I mean." I glanced back at Yeshua and Ralph in the parlor. "It'd be easier to control if the Guard comes."

"Hm. Yes, that might be wise. But we already have our patrons listed for tonight. It would be difficult to stop them."

I scowled to myself, staring down the road at the disappearing cabby. The last thing I wanted was to turn away potential patrons. "Tomorrow then."

"Yes, tomorrow. Tonight, we will continue as planned."

I agreed, inhaling the brisk wind as it flittered through the front door. Gisela squeezed my shoulder, then left me alone in the foyer, readying myself for the night ahead.

TWENTY-THREE

..- -- ...- -

That night, I opened the tavern as usual, welcoming over forty people in from both our secret Witch Tunnel and the traditional tavern entrance. They filled the building with excitement, bubbling amongst themselves with wide eyes and excitement. People spoke of the stories in hushed whispers: would they tell a story about the one-eyed prince? Or would there be a new story? What about the common tale about the Forest Queen? There were so many stories, but the night was short and sacred.

I loved the way the tavern bolstered. Patrons practiced magic in the corners of the rooms, sending sparks flying, enchanting many with their talents. Yeshua, Gisela, and Ralph sat at the front of the audience, listening to each story with intent. As always, I kept to myself, serving drinks and listening as stories turned into songs and songs turned into dances. If Ryon was here with me, I'd dance with him, but I just swayed behind the counter, humming to myself.

Often, the stories took me away through flights of fancy. I would lose myself, enamored with each tale, operating the bar in a haze. For a moment, I was a warrior fighting a dragon; another, a mere princess yearning to be saved; and in one of them, I was even a mapmaker who traveled the world. Stories have that sort of danger about them: you forget who you are and fly away.

Perhaps that was why the Order feared them.

Most days, I stayed completely swept away by these tales, only for the sunrise to wake me from my reverie.

That night, my reverie broke with a bang.

The clattering of pots and pans from upstairs pulled me out of the stories. I stumbled back, dropping one glass of liquor on the ground.

The banging continued. Everyone stopped.

My heart hung in my chest, stuck between two beats.

Another bang.

I should have listened to Elodie.

Like when Elodie discovered the tavern, I didn't hesitate. I hopped on the counter, grabbed a pot and pan, then slammed them together.

--. ---

Go.

Chaos exploded as people pushed towards the Witch Tunnel, pushing aside tables and chairs as they tried to be the first ones to leave. I ducked behind the bar to avoid the commotion.

Pow!

A gunshot exploded.

It wasn't from upstairs. It was too close.

Another gunshot.

My ears buzzed as I peeked over the top of the counter. Ralph stood in the middle of the room with pistol smoking in his hand.

Two of the storytellers lay on the ground, bleeding.

More gunshots followed. I glanced around as smoke reverberated from Ralph's barrel. Gisela and Yeshua had vanished. Did they know about Ralph? Had this been a part of an elaborate plan to take out the storytellers?

Surely not! Gisela and Yeshua told stories, too. Why would they want to see the storytellers fall?

I didn't have time to ponder it, my heartbeat rising in my ears with each passing second.

Ralph approached the counter, shoving a few storytellers out of the way. He no longer looked so small. His face was still narrow, his glasses too big, but there was an aura of strength and confidence pulsating around him.

"Up," he barked. His voice sounded deeper, too.

Where had I seen him?

I pulled myself up from behind the counter, meeting Ralph's gaze.

"Why? Why'd you... Why?" I whispered.

He pressed the pistol to my chest. "My captain's been trying to scoff out storytelling for a while. He knew you were one to cause trouble after you altered documents. Then we found that old lady on your lawn. So, he sent me undercover, had me poking and prodding. Met Gisela and Yeshua, and when I found out they had previous relations with you, I done told my boss, and we hatched a plan. Wasn't too hard." He poked me in the chest with his pistol. "Now get up. Come with me."

"And if I refuse?"

"Then you'll be dead."

I glanced around the room once more, hoping to catch Gisela or Yeshua. Or anyone. But no one looked at me, continuing to thrust their way towards the exit.

I couldn't blame them. I was just the tavern wench, after all.

With my hands raised, Ralph led me up the stairs. There, the front doors hung on their hinges, with a handful of guards sitting in my parlor led by none other than Captain Cordova himself.

"Ah, Miss Ivans. I did not think I would see you again so soon." The captain smirked. "Thank you, Lieutenant Reynolds."

Lieutenant Reynolds! Realization swung at me with a steel bat. I recognized that name! It was only uttered once, but enough for me to remember. Ralph was one of the lieutenants who entered my home after we found Brenda Harley dead on our doorstep. He almost kicked me in the face.

How had I been so blind?

Ralph bowed his head with a smirk. "Of course, sir."

I glowered at him.

Until Captain Cordova dragged my attention back with the tip of his finger. He smirked at me, his eyes as lifeless as his smile. "Now what do we do with you, Miss Ivans?"

"Just send me to the Pit like you did to Ryon already," I snapped. "You've already decided I'm guilty."

"Ah, but what good does that do? We hide you away, and another wench takes your place, isn't that right? Clearly, sending your lover to the Pit didn't hinder your determination." He shook his head, curling a strand of my hair behind my ear. "I think we need to make you into an example about what happens to storytellers."

I restrained a scream as Captain Cordova shoved me forward and pulled back my hair. One of his lieutenants forced my mouth open. His fingers tasted like metal as he pulled my tongue out of my mouth.

Captain Cordova removed a knife from his belt and pressed it onto my tongue. A pain ripped through my mouth, masked only by the flavor of blood.

"Any last words, dear? You won't be speaking again for a very long time."

"'Uck 'ou!" I spat blood at him.

"Very well. If that's the case—"

The knife slid to the center of my tongue. My head spun. Bile rose in my throat.

Then someone else spoke. "I have something to say!"

At first, I thought the blood was going to my head. Everything spun. I couldn't focus.

But I knew that voice.

Captain Cordova stopped, lifting his knife away from my mouth. "And what is a little lady like you doing here?"

"Protecting my sister."

Through tears, I met Elodie's gaze. I wanted to run to her, envelop her in a hug, and apologize for everything I had done to wrong her. Despite everything, she came back. It didn't matter that I didn't listen. She was my sister.

We were family.

"And what are you going to do, little lady? Shoot me?"

I peered past Captain Cordova at Elodie. She held a hunting rifle in her arms, shaking. "I will if I have to."

"You'll miss," the captain continued.

"No, I won't."

"Are you really going to risk your sister's life?" the captain chuckled. "Besides, threatening a Guard is a punishable offense."

"Yes...but I've been reading!"

"Reading?"

"Yes! Reading! And I happen to know that what you're doing is illegal!"

"Storytelling is illegal. You understand that, ma'am. I've seen you at my brother's services."

"Storytelling is, yes, but my sister is running an establishment! What people do here is outside her jurisdiction." Elodie cocked the rifle once. "Under Statute 19-10-20-B, storytelling is illegal on all counts, yes. But upon further investigation, under Section 16-C of the statute, only after performing a story may an individual be arrested...but *only* if witnessed by the proper authority. Owners of facilities are not liable for their patron's actions." Elodie spoke with confidence. "Have you seen my sister tell a story?"

Captain Cordova sneered. "Reynolds! Did she tell a story in your presence?"

Ralph fidgeted. "N-No, sir. She only worked the bar."

"Shite! Then...shite!" Captain Cordova still didn't loosen his grip on me.

"I suggest you leave, Captain. Or I'll be filing a formal inquiry." Elodie kept her poise.

"I recommend that this establishment closes. Otherwise, I'll have a guard coming every night until we have proof."

Elodie might have smiled. Dizziness mocked my attention. I could hardly see anymore as blood continued staining my lips. "Statute 10-12-C: Guards may not occupy private residences. And before you say anything, this house is also my sister's private residence. Yes, she is operating a tavern as a place of business. But in addendum 6-B of the statute, it says that unless a guard is there as a patron, they are considered solicitors as established in the case of *Freida's Junction v. the Rosadian Guard*. My sister, as the owner of the tavern, may deny service. The Guard may only enter with proof of illegal activities."

"We know she is running a storytelling bar!"

"You know she is operating a bar, and she has acquired the proper licenses. The only proof you have is that of a lieutenant who, if I understand correctly, had only hearsay proof in the first place."

Ralph squirmed. "I listened to the stories."

"To listen to stories is not proof, Lieutenant. Under addendum 6-C of the previously mentioned case, you do indeed need a warrant to search any private residence.

Otherwise, all evidence has been obtained under false means." Elodie smirked in my direction before continuing, "I understand that the Guard might be a bit unorthodox in its approach, but the law remains the law. And I am certain there are many advocates willing to take up my sister's case."

"We are the law!" Captain Cordova boomed.

"Then you should obey it too." Elodie approached the captain, keeping her rifle outstretched. "Now, I recommend you leave my sister alone, Captain. I have friends in high places."

Snarling, the Captain dropped me on the ground. "This isn't the end. We'll be back."

I hit the floor with a violent cough. Blood spilled from my mouth while my throat burned and roared.

"We'll see," Elodie said.

Captain Cordova called off his men, and while I couldn't see their faces, I watched as their boots marched past me out towards the field.

As soon as they vanished from my field of vision, Elodie dropped the rifle and raced to my side. She hoisted me off the ground, cradling me close, her voice no longer unwavering.

"Nan...Nan, stay with me. Please, Nanette."

"El..." I garbled her name as blood pooled on my lips.

"Don't speak. Just stay awake. Please stay awake. I can't lose you, Nan. I'm sorry. We should have never...I'm sorry, Nan."

I wanted to tell her I forgave her. I wanted to reiterate my apology. Instead, my head roared with pain from my jaw to my temples.

Spots filled my vision.

Soon, I was drifting.

TWENTY-FOUR

..- - - ....-

A cotton blanket.

A warm bed.

And a hand wrapped around mine.

I woke to birds chirping. Blinking a few times, I squinted into the daylight, my eyelids heavy. They fell again a few moments later as I tried my best to suffocate the aches in my jaw with slumber.

Only when someone pressed their lips to my forehead did my eyes flutter open.

"Nanette?"

That voice pulled me out of my fatigue. Ryon sat in a chair across from me, his hair and beard untrimmed, his skin pale, and his body composed of skin and bones.

I opened my mouth to say his name, but he held a finger to my lips, his voice raspy. "Don't speak. You're healing."

My mouth fell closed.

"Captain Cordova really messed up your tongue. The apothecary said you should be able to speak again, but it might take time." He stroked back my hair. "But you're okay."

Tears started forming in my eyes. Ryon pulled me close, holding me against his chest, whispering words of affirmation into my hair. I gripped his shirt. Was he okay? How did he get out? When? Did it matter? How long had I been asleep?

Ryon knew me well, though, and the answers came in haste. "Marietta and Elodie bought my freedom right after the events in the tavern. Marietta even negotiated my bail down slightly. They got me to the apothecary quick to deal with my sugar disease—the Guard found my vials and wasn't happy. But it's okay. I'm okay now. Without Marietta and Elodie...I don't know what would have happened to both of us."

I went to speak, but he stopped me again.

"We'll repay them, don't worry. But they had to get me out. You...you lost a lot of blood. They weren't sure if you would make it..." His eyes grew heavy. "You were feverish when they brought me back, and you kept declining. But the apothecary tried a tonic that helped with the infection. Your fever broke yesterday. And...and now you're gonna be okay. *We're* gonna be okay."

Tears welled in his eyes. I cupped his face and pressed my forehead to his, holding him there as his body quivered. My lips betrayed me. I wanted to speak, to tell him it was okay.

"I love you, Nan," he mumbled. "Once you're better, we should get married. Then we can close this damn tavern and—"

I shook my head.

"You...you want to keep it open?"

I nodded.

"What...why? After everything?"

I nodded again and glanced around my bedroom. This was home now. This was what I wanted to do.

Ryon half-smiled and squeezed my fingers. "I'm glad this hasn't dampened your spirits."

I grimaced in my attempt to smile. All I wanted was to stare at Ryon. His fingers trembled as he held me, his body moving like a living skeleton. He had sat beside me for days, but I hadn't seen him in weeks.

I thought I would never see him again.

We huddled together in silence for a while, communicating through our twisted hands and pressed forehead. Ryon usually spoke so much, but defeat made a clear home on his face. It would take a long time for him to reflect on his time in the Pit. Whatever happened, that was his story to tell. Not mine to force.

Marietta interrupted us with a knock on the door. "Oh, I am happy to see you awake, Nanette. I'll have to send word to the apothecary." She placed a tray on my lap covered with... mashed foods.

I gagged.

"I know you hate this stuff, but it's all you can eat right now, alright?" Ryon picked up a spoonful of mashed potatoes. "Open up."

I snatched the spoon from him and shoved the disgusting potatoes in my mouth.

Marietta beamed. "I really am relieved you're okay. As soon as we heard about the raids, you should have seen Elodie! She perked up out of her stupor and opened all her old law books. She found all those statutes and cases on her own. Really, she wanted to avoid any altercations with the Guard, which is why she warned you... but I guess it was too late."

I wanted to say it was my fault, I was stubborn, and I should have listened. But all I could do was bow my head in defeat.

Marietta continued, "We've been staying here for the past week while you healed. Ryon here was an utter clod during the first couple days!"

Ryon glared at Marietta.

I placed my spoon down and ran my fingers over Ryon's arm. His shoulders relaxed.

"I'm glad you two are okay. Please tell me if you need anything." Marietta said before leaving us alone again.

My thoughts raced more as our silence continued. I wanted to talk with Ryon, to have a conversation, to get him going on an obscure topic. All we had right now was the disgusting mashed meal Marietta prepared. Sure, it probably tasted fine. At least until she mashed it!

Ryon kept laughing at my expressions. The food dribbled from my mouth as I tried to eat, my tongue unable to guide it. How long until my tongue was normal? I think I missed eating more than talking.

Finally, Ryon spoke as I finished eating. "I never stopped thinking about you while I was in the Pit. It helped when you visited, but there wasn't anything much to do. They hadn't assigned me work yet, and no one really talks much at all. I dunno... It was so depressing and worn down and..." He sighed. "It was boring."

I chuckled. Only Ryon Barnes would think being imprisoned was boring!

"I didn't even have anything to read!"

I kept laughing. Such a silly man!

"Stop it!" He pouted, only further expediting my laughter. Eventually, a noise reminiscent of a donkey escaped my lips, and Ryon joined in my amusement.

But the noise attracted the attention of another.

"You shouldn't be getting her excited, Mr. Barnes," Elodie stood in the door with her arms crossed.

I glanced at her.

"Hi Nan," she smiled, "I'm glad you're okay."

There was so much I yearned to say to Elodie. "Thank you," "I'm sorry," "I don't deserve such an amazing sister," and "I love you," just to name a few.

But now was Elodie's turn to speak.

"Mr. Barnes... could I speak with Nanette... alone?" Elodie asked.

Ryon glanced at me, and I nodded. He released my fingers, then vanished into the hallway. I had a feeling he wouldn't go far, though.

Elodie paced around the room, then sat at the foot of my bed. She scowled at the remaining mashed dinner on my tray. "Ew."

I tried to smile.

"It reminds me of Ma's weird casserole she made. It always stunk."

Ah yes, her famous casserole. I forgot about that. I remembered the way its flavors and stenches waffled through our small home in Stilette. Elodie and I would run out of the house, playing in the streets for hours, hoping that by the time we got home, the meal would have gone bad.

We often failed. Ma knew our game.

Elodie's scowl vanished, her face softer. "Nanette, I'm so sorry. I should have trusted you over the words of the Order."

I dismissed her with my hand.

"No, no, I should have. You're my sister. I just so desperately wanted to fit into the Capitol. But... in doing so, I abandoned my family." She wiped her eyes. "It was pure chance that I overheard about the raids. I was at the Temple, and I wanted Elder Vic Tor to bless Lester. As I approached, I overhead him talking with his brother about the rumored storytelling bars. And... well... I had to warn you. I really thought I could convince you to close, but I didn't know they had already planted someone in the mess. Maybe if I came sooner..."

I held up my hand. Elodie couldn't blame herself for this. I wouldn't hear of it.

She met my gaze. "Lester didn't want to go to bed. I wanted to come sooner to help, but..."

Words continued to fail me. Instead, I tapped the tabletop.

.- .-.... ...- .

Alive.

Elodie stared at me, the cogs in her brain turning. "Yes, you are alive. But—"

I tapped the word again. If she hadn't shown up, I'd be dead. I would have bled out of my mouth, dying with stories on my tongue.

She needed to understand.

"Alive..." Elodie recited. "I saved you?"

I nodded.

"Nanette..." She took my hands. "I...I want to be a family. I really do. After this scare...I cannot believe how I treated you. And I can learn to accept Mr. Barnes—Ryon. He cares for you so much. I can tell. So please, let me be in your life again."

I wanted to say how the fault belonged to both of us.

So, I responded the only way I could.

I pulled her close and hugged her tight.

TWENTY-FIVE

..- - - .....

Within a week, I was back on my feet. While my tongue was still intact, it operated differently. I couldn't click it against the top of my mouth without sensitivity, and any hard words using my front consonants proved almost impossible. I resorted to beating around those words, finding ways to communicate without straining myself, using tap-code, and writing notes. The apothecary told me the words would return in time, but it would take practice.

That frustrated me, but I accepted it. After all, I could have lost my tongue entirely.

Or worse.

I used tap-code as my primary method of communication. Ryon spent hours poring over books so he might understand me without delay. Some days I still needed to resort to writing on notepads we left scattered through the tavern.

Marietta and Elodie, with their loud newborn Lester, eventually returned to their apartment in the city. I wanted them to stay, but their child was a nightmare, and while they were new parents, I was recovering. I needed sleep.

Elodie came almost every day, though, with Lester on her hip, and Marietta stopped by when she wasn't working. To my surprise, they supported my endeavor to keep the tavern open. Even though Elodie seemed hesitant, she understood that there was no stopping me. By her own count, I was stubborn as ever.

No wonder we were sisters.

Yet, we came to a mutual understanding, and our relationship was on the mend. That's all that mattered.

For the time being, though, we all agreed that for safety, the best thing to do was only operate the bed-and-breakfast. But we made plans to reopen to storytellers.

Our security measures were in place. Passwords remained.

But we added a caveat: new visitors always had to tell a story, no matter how ridiculous.

Thus, a secret member of the Guard would have to break their own code. And would they really do that?

And if they did, perhaps they would finally understand us.

About a month after the incident, Ryon and I lay in bed, practicing our kissing. That was one thing I didn't expect to have to learn again. This time, Ryon taught me, and we adjusted to suit my own abilities.

We pulled back from the kiss, smiling. Ryon cupped my cheek in his bony hand. Despite eating plenty, he struggled to gain back the weight he lost, nor abolish the constant fear in his eyes. Lash marks and scars served as a constant reminder of his time in the Pit, and his breaths struggled to find a normal rhythm.

At night, he tossed and turned, mumbling in his sleep as the nightmares tarnished his mind. He told me some of what happened: they starved him, beat him, treated him like scum, shoved him in ice, and lashed him for fun. After all that, they branded his wrist with two dark triangles, forever marking him as a criminal in the eyes of the Order. They called it a cleansing. Of what? Humanity?

They didn't take it from him.

As we lay there in bed, I met his eyes. "Ry... I 'ove you." It was one phrase I still said without trouble. So, I said it all the time.

"I love you too." He kissed my forehead.

"I wa... I... ca—" I gave up trying to pronounce what I wanted to say next. Instead, I rolled over and tapped my fingers against the end table:

.-- . / ... . --- ..- .-.. -.. / .-.. . --- .--. . -. .-.-.-

We should reopen.

I repeated the tap-code thrice to make sure Ryon understood.

"Reopen? You sure you're ready?" Ryon asked.

I nodded.

"If that is what you want, then I am with you."

I rolled over on top of him and kissed him hard. We melded together in a fit of giggles, kisses, touches, and embraces. I couldn't wait to marry him. But we both agreed that we would wait a year for everything to settle. Too much happened over the last couple months to justify marriage now.

Yet, I found myself thinking about Yeshua and Gisela. Part of my heart broke after what happened with Ralph. Neither of them returned to explain or justify. Did they know about Ralph? Did they care about me? I don't think I'll ever know. I was just a one-time flame to them, diminished to embers.

They had their own story.

Ryon and I spent the week preparing for the Grand Re-Opening of the Speakeasy. We redubbed it the Rosebud Tavern, a more appropriate title that kept suspicions more at bay. Elodie helped, much to my happiness. There was a new spark in her step, more reminiscent of when we were children. She was the child who used to tell stories with me, play make-believe, and have fun. She focused on making the tavern look pretty. While I liked our tavern, she had a whole new idea, with glowing lanterns and an array of liquors. I didn't stop her. She always had an eye for interior decorating, especially with her fancy tastes.

As she bumbled about, she kept Lester fidgeting on her hip. I admired her. Despite her clear exhaustion, she acted with determination. Even if I told her to take a break, she refused, continuing to lay out plans. Part of it, she claimed, was to make the escape easier and derail the guards. She started by placing high seated chairs and tables around the stage so it would be difficult to confirm if a storyteller or musician occupied the stage. With the purchase of a new mahogany piano, she encouraged me to hire someone to play. It'd be enough to distract people, producing confusion over the actual performance.

All of us came together on opening night. Marietta and Elodie would trade off upstairs, monitoring Lester while also entertaining the bed-and-breakfast guests. I would stand behind my counter as always, while Ryon would vet the patrons downstairs after opening the Witch Tunnel.

Our first bed-and-breakfast guest arrived as the sun brushed the edge of the trees.

When I opened the door, if my mouth didn't hurt so much, I would have screamed.

Jaida Heartz stood there, a suitcase in hand, a wide smile on her face.

"Ai-a!" I tried to pronounce her name.

"Do you have a room for a few nights?" She grinned.

I threw my arms around her, then ushered her inside my home.

As she put her suitcases in one of the guest rooms, she spoke excitedly as usual, but with a touch of sadness.

"My brother returned to Newbird's Arm and told me what happened. He's not coming back here for a while. He's going to deter the Order's forces back in Newbird's Arm, but there are already talks about replacing our Captain with someone from Knoll. They began construction on the Pit despite my complaints." Jaida frowned. "Unfortunately, this is much bigger than my brother and me. There are too many other factors at play."

"Oh..." I bowed my head in defeat.

"But!" Jaida protested and turned to me. "I am back here! I have so much news to share with you from my brother! You know the Senate voted to send Captain Cordova back to Knoll, right? They agreed the captain was out of line, not having a warrant or anything! They offered Captain Oberland his position back, but the man is enjoying retirement. So, who knows what will become of that division? Hopefully, for a while, storytelling is safe." Jaida grinned, "Which means this should be a success! People will continue telling their stories. And while of course I came back for you, dear, as I was extremely worried... I have a proposition."

I raised my eyebrows.

"If this is successful, more people will come out of the shadows to tell their stories. You cannot handle them alone, and keeping only one location will be detrimental! I say we open more of these. I have connections with plenty of tavern owners throughout the Capitol and beyond who would take part. Stories run taverns, a'ight? We could find more Witch Tunnels and alternate between different taverns. But I think it might be beneficial to your business."

I furrowed my brow, considering what she just said. It was definitely a fantastic idea. If we took the inflow away from one location, then the Guard might never know where to look.

I responded, "I be'ieve—"

She raised her hand. "You do not have to reply now, dear. It will take a lot of work and discussion."

I nodded.

"Now go back to work. I am sure you have a busy night ahead of you!" She ushered me from the room before I processed what she said.

I meandered downstairs, pondering her proposition, and joined Ryon in the basement. I didn't have time to tell him what happened. Moments after I arrived, a knock in tap-code reverberated around the room.

... - --- .-. -.-- - .. -- .

Story time.

We upped security with a secret knock and password. The knock and password changed every day. Rather than having Ryon go out to tell people, Marietta suggested we take advertisement space in the paper. We created a code, telling patrons to find the misspelled words. That would give them the password. Ryon went out once to tell people what to look for, but he would never have to do so again. This further protected us. The last thing I wanted was Ryon back in the Pit.

But even if they knew the password, they had to tell us a story upon entry, even if it was just a whisper to Ryon or me.

Soon, the bar bustled with stories and music. We capped attendance at twenty people for our opening, but that was enough to get drinks sold and laughter held. People came over to me, asking if I was okay and leaving tips worth more than their drinks. I said little; it was tiresome to reply to everyone. But every thirty minutes, Ryon bounded over and planted a kiss on my forehead, taking control of the conversation.

I listened to the stories from afar while one woman played a gentle tune on the piano. People laughed. My mind wandered.

In the end, could the Guard stop us? Stories were a part of our nature. We couldn't let them go. Just like how those with magic can't stop performing their magic tricks.

It's our version of magic.

Jaida came down eventually. She waved at me, took a glass of whiskey, then parked herself in a chair. I would consider her offer. It was a good idea. It meant we didn't have to run this tavern every night, and the Guards wouldn't know where to search!

Jaida and I didn't catch up that night. My attention turned instead to Elodie as she came down the stairs and joined me at the bar.

"You've done a good job, Nanette," she patted my hand. "I am sorry I didn't see it at first."

"I ha' help," I whispered.

"But you led the change. You kept your head high. Father would be proud."

I squeezed her hand in reassurance. "He 'ove us. Always."

"And we'll always be sisters."

"Yes bu'..." I shook my head and tapped on the counter.

... - --- .-. -.-- .-.-.- / -.-- --- ..- .-.-.-

Story. You.

"Story..." she recited. "I need to tell a story?"

I nodded. "You 'ew..."

Elodie squirmed.

"El..." I begged.

"You're right, yes, fair is fair. Fine...fine." Elodie rose from her stool and walked across the room. She glanced back at me once, uneasiness on her face.

If she did this, she would break the spell the Order had over her. It had to be scary. She wanted to fit in with Rosada after all this time. But stories were the one way to fit in with the entire world.

She only had to tell one.

Elodie sat down on the stool, her eyes never leaving me. Ryon glanced at me from his spot by the wall and raised his eyebrows. And even Jaida looked perplexed.

But I believed in Elodie.

She cleared her throat, fidgeted with her fingers, and fixated again on me. "I haven't told a story in a long time, so I apologize in advance."

Most people were too drunk to care. But I nodded. It would be okay.

So she began, "There once was a girl who set the world ablaze. Her name is Doris Nanette Ivans."

EPILOGUE

.-- . ... .-.. --- --. .-- .

I wish I could say my story was one of grandeur. I didn't change the world, but I can say I helped it. For over fifty years, I have run this tavern now, the focal point of our expansive network throughout Rosada. We are the haven for storytellers across the region, as the Order's reign has grown stronger and continues to mark those who disobey with a sign of vagrancy.

Together, Jaida and I formed our network. Elodie served with legal advice, finally putting her law degree to use. Even Marietta left work in the government to help with our finances. Ryon, to be honest, was the face of our business. He entertained guests, finding new people to fill our tavern from top to bottom. Even once his eyesight began to fail, he remained the face, always forcing a smile, even on the days when his nightmares screamed the loudest. In the end, we were self-sustaining, and while Guards had their suspicions, we always stopped their raids.

Ryon and I married a year after the attack. We never had kids. Our tavern was our child. Besides, once Elodie and Marietta moved back in with us and had three children, our lives were plenty busy. All three of her children have since taken up reigns in the tavern now that I am in my twilight years.

Nowadays, in my old age, descending the stairs every night is far too cumbersome. Instead, I sit in my chair in the parlor, collecting fees, tapping codes on the wood, and keeping an eye out for shadows on the horizon. Some nights, I sit at the top of the stairs to listen to stories and watch the array of magic brought to us. I've heard countless stories coupled with magic: from a young woman putting on a fire show to a young man using illusions to tell his wonderful tales. Where else could you witness such spectacles without fear?

My tavern is a home for many. It is my home. It was where I got married, where I watched Elodie's children grow up, and where I intend to spend the rest of my days.

I hope someday people can tell their stories without fear, just as I've told mine to you now. While my tongue has healed, I have found it easier to say this in written word or to communicate with tap-code. I've never been a great performer. Besides, no matter whether we tell or write our stories, they bring us together.

They're what keep us alive.

Even though Marietta, Elodie, Jaida, and Ryon have all passed, leaving me alone, their stories stay in this house. I see them in shadows, and I listen to them in the tales downstairs. Elodie's children talk about them to their children, and like ghosts, they never truly go away.

I may never live to see the day when storytelling is no longer outlawed. But I've done my job to keep these stories alive, so one day you may tell your story.

And if you don't know where to come, know that I have a home for you. No matter your story, no matter your background, come on by to my little tavern where ears are plenty, drinks are bountiful, and you can always speak easy.

Want more tales from the Effluvium?

The adventure continues in...

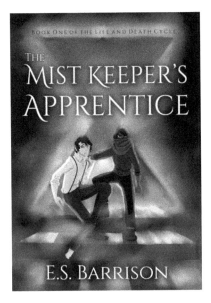

Also by E.S. Barrison...

The Life & Death Cycle
The Mist Keeper's Apprentice (Book One)
A Pool of Peony (Book Two)

The Unsought Fairytale Collection
Tuppence
Focaccia

AUTHOR'S NOTE

-.--- -.

Thank you so much for taking the time to read *Speak Easy: A Tale from the Effluvium*.

If you enjoyed this book, I would appreciate it if you could:

Review this book. Reviews are a great help to an author. If you enjoyed this book, please consider leaving a review on Amazon or Goodreads.

Tell Others. When you share this book with others on social media, you're allowing others to discover this story. Word-of-mouth is one of the best sources of marketing for an author.

Connect with me. If you want to find out about my upcoming releases, stop by my website at www.esbarrison-author.com. Or connect with me on social media.

Thank you!

E.S. Barrison

ACKNOWLEDGMENTS

- .... .- -. -.- ...

To all the following, my thanks, for your support, friendship, and kindness throughout this process:

First, as always, to Matthew, thank you for dealing with all the craziness I put you through. Also, thank you for reading literally every one of my stories...it means so much.

Next, to my beta readers, for all your valuable insights to make this book the best possible.

Of course, I must thank my editor, Charlie, not only for helping me polish this story, but also by helping me develop proper representation in this book.

And finally, to you, my readers, who give each story I write a chance.

Thank you again.

E.S. Barrison

ABOUT THE AUTHOR

.- -... --- ..- -

E.S. Barrison has been writing and creating stories for as long as she can remember. After graduating from the University of Florida, she has spent the past few years wrangling her experiences to compose unique worlds with diverse characters. Currently, E.S. lives in Orlando, Florida with her family.